P.S. I LOATHE YOU

P.S. I LOATHE YOU

A CLIQUE NOVEL BY
LISI HARRISON

poppy

LITTLE, BROWN AND COMPANY
New York   Boston

"Need U Bad" by Melissa A. Elliott, Cainon Renard Lamb, Taurian John Osbourne, David W. Sinclair, Nicholas Taylor Stanton, Jazmine Sullivan (EMI April Music, Inc., Itation Records, Roynet Music, Universal Music-Z Tunes, LLC). All rights reserved.

Poppy

Little, Brown and Company
Hachette Book Group
237 Park Avenue, New York, NY 10017
For more of your favorite series, go to www.pickapoppy.com

First Edition: February 2009

Poppy is an imprint of Little, Brown Books for Young Readers.
The Poppy name and logo are trademarks of Hachette Book Group, Inc.

The characters and events in this book are fictitious. Any similarity to real persons, living or dead, is coincidental and not intended by the author.

Cover design by Andrea C. Uva
Cover photos by Roger Moenks
Author photo by Gillian Crane

Produced by Alloy Entertainment
151 West 26th Street, New York, NY 10001

ISBN: 978-0-316-00680-11

10 9 8 7 6 5 4 3 2 1
CWO
Printed in the United States of America

CLIQUE novels by Lisi Harrison:

THE CLIQUE

BEST FRIENDS FOR NEVER

REVENGE OF THE WANNABES

INVASION OF THE BOY SNATCHERS

THE PRETTY COMMITTEE STRIKES BACK

DIAL L FOR LOSER

IT'S NOT EASY BEING MEAN

SEALED WITH A DISS

BRATFEST AT TIFFANY'S

THE CLIQUE SUMMER COLLECTION

P.S. I LOATHE YOU

If you like THE CLIQUE, you may also enjoy:

The **Poseur** series by Rachel Maude
The **Secrets of My Hollywood Life** series by Jen Calonita
Footfree and Fancyloose by Elizabeth Craft and Sarah Fain
Betwixt by Tara Bray Smith
Haters by Alisa Valdes-Rodriguez

For Kevy. P.S. I Love You.

A plaguelike swarm of pigeons, the same milky color as the overcast sky, circled above the Pretty Committee. Their flapping wings sounded like the crisp snap of a magician's cape. Their phlegmmy cooing reached a frenzied pitch. And they unleashed their watery white poo on the fuel-efficient cars below them with remarkable precision.

In movies, opening scenes like these often suggest something eerie is approaching. That a menacing force is gathering strength. That a curse is looming. That the natural order is being disrupted . . .

But Massie Block knew better.

"Ehma—*Ewww.*" She stopped walking to wave a drifting feather away from her face.

Alicia, Dylan, and Kristen stopped too.

"This is so Briarwood's fault." Massie pinch-tightened her gold silk scarf, wiping her leather leggings clean of any bird essence.

"How's this pigeon infestation *Briarwood's* fault? What did *they* do?" Alicia adjusted her unsightly pink New York Yankees cap.

"Relax." Massie cupped Alicia's shoulder with more force than a shoulder-cupping called for. "I'm nawt saying it's *Josh's* fault. The only thing I blame him for is that hat."

"Massie's right." Kristen twirled her shark-tooth necklace. "The kitchen scraps have more than doubled since the boys moved in." She gestured to the wall of wide metal Dumpsters that lined the far side of the faculty parking lot. "It's a dirty-bird buffet."

"All you can *tweet*," Dylan giggle-added.

Massie sighed, no longer in the mood for seventh-grade jokes. She had waited all weekend to make fun of the ex-crushes in their trailer classrooms and wanted to get there before Claire did. It was bad enough Claire had turned down carpool to double on Cam's bike. For her to scoop the "Ex-Crushes Banished to Tiffany Box Trailers" story would be unbearable.

"Form-a-*tion*!" Massie thundered. An asphalt-pecking klatch of pigeons flapped their wings in panic and flew en masse to the far side of the lot.

The girls quickly lined up on either side of their alpha, awaiting further instruction from her purple Marc Jacobs Mouse flats. As soon as she lifted the left one off the pavement, they synchronized, then launched. Within seconds the Pretty Committee picked up speed, charging the parking lot like the Radio City Rockettes in a cutthroat game of Red Rover.

Destination: the two distant trailers behind the maple trees where the terrified birds had just landed.

The same trailers Principal Burns had tried to pawn off as "overflow facilities" when the Briarwood boys had crashed OCD. The same ones the Pretty Committee had been sent to—*with* the LBRs—thanks to a devious plan hatched by ex-Derrington and the other soccer boys. The *saaaame* ones Massie had made over into glam, supersize Tiffany boxes and eventually unloaded back onto the exes. Sure the trailers cleaned up well, but just like an LBR after a department-store makeover, one good scrub and they were back to their ghastly old selves again.

"I can't wait to see how funny the wannabe-Beckham boys look in robin's egg–blue classrooms with glitter-cotton walls, mirrored desks, and vanilla-scented room spray." Massie grinned, the light breeze heightening the sensitivity of her Whitestripped teeth.

"They'll still be Beckhams," Kristen deadpanned. "Just Victorias instead of Davids." She cackled.

"Point!" Alicia smacked the side-view mirror of a white Infiniti as they sailed past it.

Massie stopped suddenly. "Ew! Smell that?" She lifted her Chanel No. 19–scented wrist to her nose for relief. But the parmesan cheese/rotten lettuce/cat food stench emanating from the pigeon-infested Dumpsters could not be avoided.

Screeching to a halt, the others lifted their shirts to their noses and inhaled their powder-scented deodorants.

"Gawd." Massie jammed her winter white Juicy Rock the Bag tote against her ribs, protecting it like a puppy in a hurricane. "If I wanted to go to school with trash I'd be at Abner Doubleday Day."

"Let's sue!" Alicia lifted her index finger and strut-blocked Dylan's path.

Dylan sidestepped Alicia and giggle-lifted her Starbucks cup to avoid Mr. Myner's pine green Chevy Tahoe hybrid.

"Ahhhh!" she yelped as the plastic top popped off. Latte splashed all over her white Joie henley dress. "Leeeeesh!"

The girls jump-backed away from Dylan's chai-soaked wrist.

"What did *I* do?" Alicia squealed.

"You body-checked me into Myner's truck." Dylan whipped the empty cup through his open window.

"Where was I *supposed* to go?" Alicia stomped her camel-colored Kate Spade flat against the asphalt. "*Someone* insisted we walk in formation."

"What's wrong with *formation*?" Massie flicked Alicia's shiny black ponytail.

"Nothing." Alicia steadied her swinging hair. "It's just that walking side by side isn't the best idea when you're sur-rounded by cars covered in pigeon butt—"

"Can everyone puh-*lease* focus on *me* for a minute?" Dylan pulled the soaked brown cotton off her belly. "I look like I'm wearing used toilet paper."

The girls burst out laughing.

"It's the opposite of funny!" Dylan's green eyes began to moisten.

"Here." Kristen held out her floral-print canvas Roxy bag.

"How's *last* summer's beach bag gonna help?"

"Open it," Kristen insisted.

Dylan lifted her sunglasses and peered inside. Kristen's G-rated, mom-approved outfit was crumpled in a pathetic reject heap. As usual, she'd worn it out of her condo, and then Range Rover–replaced it with something sexier—generally handed down from one of the other girls. Today it was blue-and-black plaid wool short shorts, a gray V-neck bell-sleeve sweater, and knee-high black moccasins.

"What am I gonna to do with baggy navy cords and a white turtleneck?" Dylan handed the bag to Kristen. "Crash third-grade picture day?"

"Your call, Cottonelle." Kristen hooked the Roxy over her shoulder.

"Hehhhhhhhhhh, hoooooooooo. Hehhhhhhhhhh, hoooooooooo. Heeeeeeeee, hoooooooooooooooooooooooooooooooooooooooooo."

A low-flying pigeon hovered above their heads, flapping its wings but not moving, like it was treading water.

"Hehhhhhhhhhh, hooooooooooooooooooooooooooooooooooo," it announced, then quickly flew away.

"Ahhhhhh!" Dylan shouted at her shoulder. "I've been tagged!"

Students lazily making their way toward the BOCD main building turned and stared. Passing boys on their way to the overflow trailers snickered. The Pretty Committee burst into hysterics.

"It's nawt funny!" Dylan giggle-cry-shrieked.

"Ahhhhh!" Alicia wailed. "It got me too!" She lifted her thigh and wiped her splotched gray Ralph Lauren skinny jeans on the door of a black Prius.

Massie grabbed a passing LBR by the arm, ripped the black, fake-Prada backpack off her shoulder, and held it over her own head.

The curly-headed blonde was too shocked to speak. Instead, she glared at Massie, her wide brown eyes begging for an explanation.

"*Buh-lieve* me." Massie fart-waved her away with a dismissive shoo. "I'll give it back once I'm inside."

"Strike three!" Kristen shook her arm, but it was too late. The *fly-arrhea* had already seeped into the wool fibers of her gray sweater.

She reached for her bag. "Ineedmyclothesback."

Dylan yanked it away. "You said *I* could wear them!"

"That was *before* I got hit!"

Dylan jumped back. "Sorry." She hugged the quilted floral bag to her chest. "I need to pull a bag borrow-and-steal."

Massie laughed from the safety of her Frauda canopy.

"No way!" Kristen gasped. "Those are *my* clothes!"

"You already *have* a crush," Dylan pouted. "And he won't be back at school for another week. So who cares what you wear?"

"Point." Alicia lifted her finger in support of Dylan. "I have Josh, Claire has Cam, Massie has Dempsey, and you have Dune. Dylan is the only *C-minus*. She needs all the help she can get."

Suddenly, everyone was silent, each girl wondering if *she* was the only one on the outside of the inside joke.

The wheels in Massie's head spun like a Ferrari's. *I ended the boyfast. . . . Now everyone is allowed to have a crush . . . and everyone does. . . . Well, nawt everyone . . . Poor Dylan is more boyless than Lindsay Lohan on date night but . . . Ehmagawd . . . Got it!!*

Massie's dark eyebrows shot up. Her amber eyes widened. Her glossy lips parted. "C-*minus*! *Crush* minus. Without crush. *Right*?"

"Given." Alicia nodded. "I knew you'd get it."

Massie cocked her head and half smiled. "I knew I would too."

"Fine, C-Minus, keep 'em," Kristen muttered to Dylan. Then she rolled back her shoulders. "Who knows? This may be just what you need."

"LBR clothes?" Massie crinkled her nose.

"No, the *poo*." Kristen giggled. "I heard getting pigeon-painted was good luck."

"Funny." Massie eyed the boys gathering at the end of the parking lot. "You don't *look* so lucky." She rolled back her shoulders and picked up her pace.

Her friends' proud smiles faded like Mystic tans.

BOCD's majestic brick building and its highly perfumed student body were well behind them. Now the overflowing trash bins were only steps away, and the parmesan cheese/rotten lettuce/cat food smell had become unbearable.

Massie dry-heaved. "Activate face cover in three . . . two . . . one . . . annnnd *go!*" She jammed her gold scarf into her nostrils then ushered the Pretty Committee past what resembled the set of *WALL*E*.

"Diiiieeeeeeeeeeee, dirty birrrrrrrrrrds!"

Bloated pigeons unclamped their pink talons from rusty bins and panic-flapped to safety.

"Wait for meeee!" Alicia called, her face buried under her black-and-white striped cashmere tunic.

"Over'ere!" Massie whisper-barked once she hit grass, signaling her troops to join her behind the thick trunk of a maple tree. Cautiously lowering her scarf, she nose-sipped the air. "Ahhhhh." She sighed with relief. "Much better."

The parmesancheeserottenlettucescatfood smell had dissipated. But the crisp Alpine spring water scent of OCD was hardly back. Something new had taken its place. Something fragrant. Something Christmassy . . . Something . . .

"Ehma-*pine*," Massie gasped, her eyes lifted to the sky.

Kristen, Alicia, and Dylan stared up in amazement, their glossy lips shaped like Cheerios. Hundreds of green, tree-shaped air-fresheners, the kind sold at gas stations and suburban mini-marts, dangled from the branches of the maple. They twirled and swayed in the breeze, creating small flickering shadows over the girls' designer footwear.

"Look!" Dylan whipped off her dVbs and widened her emerald green eyes. Her gaze led them to the *ex*–Tiffany box trailers.

"What did they *do*?" Massie's heart sank to her knees. A moment later it sank to her Mouse flats. Then it sank all the way to China.

Beyond the pine-scented maples were two freshly painted *white* trailers. Both were covered by black tarp canopies that provided enough shade for the—

"Soccer videos?" Kristen blurted, her eyes darting across the outside of Trailer No. 1, which showed Landon Donovan kicking the ball to Beckham. Trailer No. 2 featured EA's FIFA 09 video game, which Josh Hotz and Kemp Hurley were playing with fight-to-the-finish intensity.

"Ohhhh!" the spectators roared when Josh blocked Kemp's shot.

"Seriously?" Alicia removed her pink crush-cap. "Josh was a total text maniac this weekend and never said a word." Her dark brown eyes practically filled with little thumping hearts. "Impressive."

"Who did they hire?" Massie hate-glared at the projectors fastened to the branches of the nearby maple.

"Bill Gates," Kristen stated confidently, staring at the A/V setup.

"Puh-lease," Massie snapped. "It's not *that* impressive."

"Oh no, I meant—" Kristen stopped and blushed, as if she had accidentally revealed something she shouldn't have. "I meant Danh Bondok probably did it."

"*Who*?" Alicia and Massie giggle-asked at the same time.

Kristen finally took her eyes off the Galaxy game and focused on the conversation. "I mean Candy Corn."

"Candy Corn the LBR?" Alicia looked at Massie, silently asking her if such a thing were possible. "That yellow-toothed guy?"

Massie shrugged.

"The one we just made over?"

"Yes, Candy Corn the yellow-toothed LBR," Kristen said with a trace of impatience. Or was it defensiveness? "His *real* name is Danh Bondok and he's a tech genius. He could do this in his sleep."

"Bonnn-dock," Dylan burped.

Everyone laughed except Massie. "How do you know him?"

Kristen blushed again. "Um, he's on scholarship too, so we just kinda met that way, I guess."

"Whatevs." Massie sighed, fighting the urge to run home backwards, get into bed, and start the morning all over again.

"Can you believe this?" a familiar voice chirped.

The girls turned to see Claire and Cam coasting toward them on a black Electra bike with thick fat tires and dark green spokes. Legs lifted out in front of them, matching silver helmets tilted left, they smiled brighter than the bike's reflectors. Their fight was ah-bviously over, and they were back together. *Forever.*

If they had been actors in a movie, Massie would have thought they looked enviably ah-dorable. But because Claire was her friend, and clearly way happier than Massie was, Massie wanted to knock them both to the ground.

The day was *nawt* supposed to start like this. Nawt at *awll*. Claire wasn't supposed to ditch carpool so she could bike to school with Cam. Birds weren't supposed to destroy their post-boyfast outfits. The soccer boys weren't supposed to make over the Tiffany box trailers. And the Pretty Committee was nawt, nawt, *nawt* supposed to be impressed.

Massie suddenly felt like she was trying to turn a door handle with overmoisturized hands. Her grip was slipping. And she was starting to panic.

"Why are you hiding?" Cam slammed on the brakes.

Claire stepped off the bike, unclipped her helmet, and shook out her blond hair like some Italian supermodel shooting a Vespa ad.

"We're nawt hiding," Massie explained to Cam's one blue eye, which matched his navy sweatshirt in a distracting sort of way. "We were, um, waiting for you guys. This is where we decided to meet. Right, Kuh-laire?"

Luckily Claire nodded, untangling the knot in Massie's stomach and turning it into a smile. Despite her reconciliation with Cam, she still had Massie's back.

"If you wouldn't mind excusing us"—Massie smirked at Cam, this time looking into his green eye, just to show she had no real preference—"we have some Pretty Committee business to take care of."

"No prob." Cam saluted, his wheels already angled toward the heated match between Josh and Kemp. "Going to the game tonight?" he asked, mostly to Claire, who was snapping her helmet around his handlebars.

"Soccer?"

He giggle-nodded in a "what else would I be talking about" sort of way. "We're playing the Maverick School Groundhogs. And MSG plays hard."

Claire turned to Massie, lifting her blond brows with hope.

"Opposite of yes." Massie twirled her eighty-four-day-old purple hair streak. "We're going to Dylan's to do some online shopping."

"Sounds fun!" Cam said sarcastically as he high-fived Claire and rode off to greet his friends.

"*Shopping*?" Claire stomped a red Converse All Star, unable to hide her disappointment. "Don't you want to hang out with Dempsey after school?"

"He's not into soccer." Massie swiped her lips with devil's food cake–flavored Glossip Girl. "He's an actor," she said with a trace of a British accent. "And he got a call back for the *Wizard of Claus*. For the Wizard."

"So you're still into Dempsey?" Kristen smacked a pine air-freshener.

Massie cocked her head to the side. "Why *wouldn't* I be?"

"I dunno." Kristen shrugged. She bit her thumbnail before pressing on. "So how much do you like him? You know, out of ten?"

"Ten," Massie insisted. "Times ten."

Just then Layne Abeley and her alt-to-a-fault friend Meena strolled by belting out the song "Popular" from *Wicked*. And for some reason Kristen kind of half smiled at Layne when she passed. It had to be pity, because she was singing about something she'd never experience . . . well, either that or gas.

"So basically you'd be upset if someone else liked him and he liked them back?"

Massie leaned closer, her amber eyes fixed and serious. "Have you heard something?"

"No," Kristen blurted. "Why, have you?"

"*No!*"

"You know, *she's* auditioning." Kristen tilted her head toward Layne. "Doesn't that tell you something about how *un* the play is?"

"What's wrong with *Layne*?" Claire snapped.

"Nothing." Kristen blushed. "It's just that I . . . I thought maybe it would be cooler if you crushed on a guy who's into sports, nawt middle-school *theater*."

Massie squint-looked into Kristen's green eyes as if trying to read something blurry. Since when had Kristen become so concerned with Massie's public image? Kristen was her poor friend, not her PR friend. Who had suddenly given her permission to drop those two essential *o*'s?

"Um, are you saying actors are nawt hawt?" Massie hissed.

"Kinda." Kristen lifted her blond brows in a "truth hurts" sort of way.

"Have you ever heard of Zac?"

"Yeah, but—"

"Hayden?"

"Yeah, b—"

"Hartnett?

"Ye—"

"Chace? Penn—"

"*Okay!*" Kristen held up her hand. "It's just that you said we could *like* boys this week, so I assumed we'd be hanging at the game after school. Not shopping."

"Point." Alicia lifted her French-manicured finger as she watched Josh high-five Cam.

"We *do* like boys this week," Massie insisted. "Just nawt soccer."

Just then the boys began laugh-chanting her ex-crush's name.

"Derr-ing-ton! Derr-ing-ton! Derr-ing-ton!"

Massie immediately blushed. The Pretty Committee was studying her, ah-bviously wondering if she had any last drops of crush left in her, like an upside-down can of Diet Coke that continued to drip soda even when it was empty.

"Ew, puh-lease!" Massie rolled her eyes and snorted like a sleepy piglet. "I'm over him times ten times *twenty*!"

"Good." Alicia began walking. "Then let's go see what that's all about."

"Hold!" Massie swiped more Glossip Girl across her lips,

then licked. Sugary sweetness coated her tongue and instantly lifted her mood. "Focus! I have an announcement to make."

The Pretty Committee formed a tight circle under the pine-scented maple, each girl resisting the urge to peek at the boys.

"*Derr-ing-ton! Derr-ing-ton! Derr-ing-ton!*"

Massie cleared her throat, even though it was already clear. "Last week I declared a boyfast and it almost tore us apart." Her voice was somber.

The girls nodded in agreement.

"And you know why it didn't work?"

"Because Alicia hung out with Josh behind our backs?" Dylan blurted.

"Go *flush* yourself, Cottonelle!" Alicia snapped.

Dylan folded her arms across her brown-stained henley and huff-turned to face the boys.

"*Derr-ing-ton! Derr-ing-ton! Derr-ing-ton!*"

Everyone else turned too, except Massie. Her ex was ah-bviously doing *something* silly to get her attention, and she refused to fall for the childish trick.

"The *maaaain* reason boyfast didn't work," she half yelled to recapture her friends' attention, "is because we're hawt times ten! We have ah-mazing personalities! And *most* of us have incredible style!" She lifted her eyebrow at Claire, who looked at her primary-red sneakers in shame. "And it was wrong for me to think that boys could resist us. They're only human, after all."

The girls nodded in agreement once again.

"So I have prepared a pledge poem that will put us back on the right path." She reached into her winter white Juicy tote and pulled out five platinum Coach key chains. Each one had five purple patent-leather letters dangling off the end: BFFWC. Massie thumbed open the dog-leash clip and hooked it onto the strap of her bag, then handed them out, waiting while everyone else did the same.

"I know I promised you bracelets, but I saw Strawberry and Kori at the mall buying you-know-whats. So I switched it up at the last minute." She smirked, then tapped the screen of her new iPhone 3G. "Now check your texts."

The girls quickly reached inside their bags, their BFFWC charms swinging about.

"Does everyone have the new pledge poem?"

They consulted their in-boxes and nodded.

"Good." Massie grinned. "Then grab your charms and let's recite together in three . . . two . . . one . . ."

The girls began:

We swore off boys for ten whole days,
But it didn't work so well.
We acted like backstabbing clichés—
Ehmagawd! Boyfast was hell.

But we forgave one another;
Now we're back in the groove.
Sisters, lock up your brothers,
Because we're on the move!

This time we'll do it right:
Our friendships come first.
PC support, day or night,
Or that member will be cursed.

So I hereby decree,
As my open heart gushes,
We are now BFFWC,
Best Friends Forever With Crushes!

"Yayyyyyyyy!" the girls giggle-shouted, then exchanged a round of hugs, with Massie in the center.

Everything felt right again. Their bond was Teflon-strong.

"Derr-ing-ton! Derr-ing-ton! Derr-ing-ton!"

"Who's ready to find out what all the chanting is about?"

"Meeeee!" Five hands shot into the pine-scented air.

Massie smiled proudly, ready to introduce her new leather leggings to the opposite sex.

This time the Pretty Committee would do it right. This time they would have it all.

"Derr-ing-ton! Derr-ing-ton! Derr-ing-ton!"

Like a supermodel bursting onto a runway amid a cloud of dry ice, Massie led the girls toward the chanting, as if it were all for them. She stepped over Cam's bike, which lay, wheel still spinning, on a clump of discarded backpacks. All she needed was a snappy one-liner to announce their arrival.

Hmmm . . . Something about going to school in a trailer park . . . or how they'll need a can opener to get into their new classrooms.

Nope. She didn't quite have it yet.

"Derr-ing-ton! Derr-ing-ton! Derr-ing-ton!"

Luckily, the boys were so drawn to the maple tree on their right, they didn't notice the Pretty Committee standing—

"Ehma—*butt*!" Massie smacked Alicia's shoulder. "Look!"

Dylan burst out laughing.

Derrington was perched six feet off the ground, squatting on a branch like an ape, with his Volcom jeans around his knees. He was shaking his Paul Frank boxer briefs in front of the projector lens and casting a butt-shaped shadow on Trailer No. 1. The leaves of the maple shook and his friends acted like amused monkeys.

The LBRs who shared the trailers with the soccer boys

ignored him. Instead, they mounted the metal steps to their portable classrooms like court-bound celebrities determined to escape the swarming press.

"*Magawd*, he'll do anything to get my attention," Massie muttered to herself. "What did I ever see in him?"

Alicia shook her ponytail from side to side like she had no idea.

"Thank Gawd I like Dempsey now. Double thank Gawd that he'll be in the main building with us. And triple thank Gawd that he's not into soccer."

"You hardly even *know* Dempsey." Kristen kicked a rock with her black moccasin.

"Hey, Claire!" Layne called from an open window in Trailer No. 1. "Look!" She stuck out a red fingerless–gloved hand and pinched Derrington's butt-shadow. Claire and Dylan cracked up while Massie searched Kristen's green eyes for an explanation—something that might explain why she was so anti-Dempsey. But Kristen's lashes fluttered innocently, revealing nothing.

Massie was the first to break. "Um, are you the OCD Sirens' goalie?"

"No! I'm the *captain*," Kristen snapped.

"Then why are you trying to block my shot?"

"I'm nawt." Kristen side-glanced at Layne, who was now spanking Derrington's butt-shadow. "It's just that Dempsey used to be an LBR."

"So was Leighton Meester." Massie shrugged. "She was born in jail."

"He's friends with Layne," Kristen tried again.

"So is Kuh-laire."

"You called him Humpty Dempsey for an entire year. *Re-mem-ber?*"

"Yeah, yeah, yeah." Massie waved the argument away like the smell of burnt microwave popcorn. "But he was cured of his LBR-thritis." Her body purred recalling the day she had first beheld Dempsey 2.0.

He had just returned from summering in Africa. Rugged safari-colored clothes clung to his new muscles like a hug, each crease on his distressed leather messenger bag probably representing an orphan he had read to. And confidence seeped from his tanned skin like two thousand–dollar Clive Christian cologne. His caramel blond highlights were natural. His army green eyes were supernatural. And she could feel his smile as if it were inside her belly. Dempsey Solomon was the ultimate comeback story. She was his ultimate comeback prize. And if Kristen had a problem with—

"You always told us LBR-thritis couldn't be cured, only treated," Kristen hissed.

"Um, are you forgetting the J.T. clause?" Massie hissed back.

Kristen folded her arms across her gray sweater, turned toward Trailer No. 2, and sighed. "Guess so," she huffed.

Alicia, Dylan, and Claire were starting to inch toward the boys. A few more seconds and they'd be mingle-flirting without her. This conversation had to end. Now.

"TheJ.T.clauseistheJustinTimberlakeclauseremember?"

Kristen shrugged.

Massie took a deep breath, held it for five seconds, then exhaled slowly. "We never thought Justin was hot until Cameron dated him. And we *never* thought he was a ten until he dumped her. And now he's an alpha male for life."

"So you're Cameron? Is that what you're saying?" Kristen folded her arms across her chest.

Massie shrugged in a "you said it, I didn't" sort of way.

"Derr-ing-ton! Derr-ing-ton! Derr-ing-ton!"

And then it hit her. "*He* put you up to this, didn't he? He's jealous of Dempsey and scared he'll never get me back and—"

"Dylan! Dylan! Dylannn!"

Massie whip-turned toward the shouting.

Dylan was standing below the maple, poking Massie's ex-crush's butt with a stick, like a marshmallow over a campfire. Everyone was laughing, but no one found it funnier than Derrington. Massie searched for Claire and Alicia, wondering why they didn't have the good sense to stop Dylan. But they were with Cam and Josh, playing some soccer video game on Trailer No. 2, pretending to care about their scores.

"Dylan, stop!" Massie shout-ran toward the stick in Dylan's hand. "We don't like him anymore."

"Ms. Marvil, what are you *doing*?" shouted an angry female voice that wasn't Massie's.

"Getting the stick out of his butt." Dylan snickered at Derrington's boxers, ah-bviously not realizing who she was talking to.

The boys burst out laughing while Derrington yanked up his Volcoms.

"*Excuse* me?" the voice screeched.

"Ms. Dunkel?" Dylan's cheeks turned so purple they clashed with her red hair. The matronly trailer teacher finger-pushed her big round glasses against the bridge of her nose. Tapping one square-toed, square-heeled pump, she folded her arms across her wheat-colored cardigan and nostril-sighed.

Quickly, the boys began gathering their backpacks. The Pretty Committee raced to Massie's side. And while Ms. Dunkel's head was turned, Dylan giggle-poked Derrington one last time. Then . . .

Crack.

Snap.

Thud.

The branch suddenly broke, and Derrington plummeted six feet, landing ankle-first on the yellowing grass. Like in a CSI chalk drawing, his left leg was bent and his right was straight.

Everyone gathered around.

"Give him room!" Ms. Dunkel pleaded.

The concern-furrow in her brow became an anger-furrow. The dent in her forehead was deep enough to store loose change.

"Dylan and Derrick." The teacher stood, wiping her knees. "You know what else starts with *D*?" She tapped her chin reflectively.

"Dunkel?" Derrington peeped from the ground.

Dylan cracked up.

"De-tention!" she barked. "Meet me in the faculty parking lot after school for a very special assignment." The corners of her mouth curled with delight. "Now, the rest of you, get to class." She checked her silver-plated Fossil watch. "The bell is about to ring."

The crowd dispersed, and the Pretty Committee made their way back to the main building like famished, blistered supermodels after New York's Fashion Week.

"Looks like shopping at Dylan's after school is canceled," Massie groaned. The Coach BFFWC key chains knocked against the girls' handbags as they hurried to keep up with Massie's agitated pace.

Dylan sighed. "I'm so sorry, you guys. I didn't mean to—"

"Does this mean we get to go to the soccer game?" Claire's blue eyes widened with hope.

"Opposite of yes," Massie snapped.

"You can come to my place," Kristen offered.

"Why?" Massie raised her right eyebrow. "Did you just get five computers?"

"No." Kristen shifted her weight from one moccasin to the other. "But we can share. It'll be fun."

"*Cher* is something my mom works out to, and it doesn't look like *fun*."

Massie picked up her pace even more as they entered the bird-infested parking lot.

"You never come to my house," Kristen whined.

"Because it's nawt a *house*," Massie insisted. "It's a condo."

Just then another load of fly-arrhea fell from the sky.

"My sleeve!" Kristen gripped her soiled gray sweater.

The girls giggled in spite of themselves.

"Why so sad? Pigeon poo is good luck, right?" Massie smirked.

Kristen lifted her chin and forced a smile. "Right."

"Good." Massie triple-patted her on the back. "Maybe that means you'll get a house soon."

Kristen gasped. Alicia, Claire, and Dylan glared at Massie like she had gone too far. But so what if she had? All morning, she'd felt her alpha-grip slipping. And when that happened, the only thing to do was force it back into place.

CURRENT STATE OF THE UNION

IN	OUT
Dempsey	Derrington
The Pooey Committee	The Pretty Committee
Alpha-slip	Alpha-grip

Despite everyone's best efforts to get her to stay for the soccer game, Massie convinced them to go to Pinkberry. And that meant Dylan would be missing the day's gossip download *and* Cap'n Crunch–covered fro-yo.

But once the rest of the Pretty Committee pulled away in the Blocks' Range Rover, a teensy part of Dylan felt free. After all, it wasn't every day she had a date with a boy in the faculty parking lot.

So what if the "boy" was Massie's ex-crush? Double so what if their "date" was really a detention. And triple so what if Ms. Dunkel would be there too? C-minuses can't be choosers.

Derrington was sitting on the hood of a cherry red Subaru Forester listening to his black iPod nano when Dylan arrived. The laces on his left sneaker were untied and the tongue had been lifted, like a CEO who loosens his tie after a stressful day at the office. The guy was so hawt he made a foot injury look cool.

"Is Dunkel here yet?" she whispered, just in case.

Derrington shook his head and drummed on his thigh. An ah-dorable mess of dirty blond hair flopped against the green frames of his Ray-Bans.

Dylan grinned. Their sunglasses were the same color.

Then she frowned.

Why hadn't she put on a fresh coat of lip gloss? Why hadn't she swapped out Kristen's ugly cords for something more flattering from the lost-and-found? Why had she eaten chive cream cheese for lunch when it repeated on her like a senile grandmother?

Dylan scanned faculty parking. School had ended almost thirty minutes ago and the lot was still full.

"Were the teachers abducted?" she joked, then immediately hated herself for not being funny.

Derrington continued drumming.

Dylan plucked the thin wire from his ear and—

"AHHHHHH!" he screamed in her face.

"AHHHHHHHHHHHHHHHH!" She jumped back.

He burst out laughing, waving his nano to show it was never really on. "Gotcha!"

"You scared me!" Dylan smacked his foot.

"AHHHHHH!" he shouted again. Only this time he was biting his lower lip and grabbing his ankle.

"Ehmagawd, I'm sooo sorry." She covered her mouth with two hands, realizing she'd just smacked his bum foot.

"S'fine." He winced.

"Here." Dylan pulled the poo- and coffee-stained henley out of her bag and began wrapping it around his swollen ankle.

"OW!" he shouted again. "What are you dooo-ing?"

"Applying direct pressure. Now stay still." She swatted his hand away, imagining they were characters in a movie. He was the testy, wounded tough guy, about to realize he needed the touch of a beautiful woman to complete him.

"I'm not *bleeding*!" He shouted like he was mad but smiled like he was charmed. "I have a sprained—"

"Off my car!" Ms. Dunkel hurried toward them, waving her hands like she was walking through spiderwebs.

Derrington slid off the SUV, landing on his good foot. The other one hovered above the asphalt, like Heather Mills in a high heel. "Sorry." He snapped his head, flipping the blond shaggy hair off his face. Dylan inched to his side, feeling electricity pass between their fingers, which were almost touching. Could he feel it too?

"As you can see, pigeons have had their way with our vehicles." Ms. Dunkel surveyed the streaked cars like an army general assessing casualties. "Sewwwww"—she put her hands in the pockets of her navy Dockers and rocked back on her square heels—"for the next two days, while the faculty attends a BOCD overpopulation summit, you will scrub our cars clean. And in the future, you will do your best to fight all urges to climb trees, drop your drawers, and poke each other with sticks on school property."

Dylan and Derrington exchanged side-glances, fighting the giggles as the details of their mission were explained.

"Understood?"

They nodded yes.

"A member of the custodial staff is on the way with biodegradable soap, water, cloths, buckets, and paper hats."

"Paper hats?" Dylan smoothed her red curls, apologizing to them in advance.

"Yes, paper hats." Ms. Dunkel pointed at the gray sky as

if that should explain everything. "There is a fair amount of disease in bird feces. If it seeps into your scalp, it may have unfavorable consequences."

"Good ta know." Derrington lifted his brows in faux fascination.

"Yes." Ms. Dunkel turned toward the squeaking wheels of the incoming janitor's cart.

"Here?" grunted a pale, freckle-faced man with a tight blond Afro the same color as his wannabe–Stella McCartney flight suit.

"Thank you, Russell." Ms. Dunkel nodded dismissively. "And good luck, students." She double-tapped the supply cart like it was a horse, then turned and hurried off toward the main building, her square heels scraping across the pavement.

"How are we gonna do this?" Dylan whined. "Should we sub it out and hire someone?"

Derrington snickered as if she were joking. "You have an iPod?"

"New iPhone," she bragged.

A pigeon phlegm-cooed above their heads.

"Y'ave Nickelback?" Derrington grabbed two paper hats.

Dylan shook her head no twice: once for Nickelback and again for the paper hat. Fashion trumped feces.

"Coldplay?"

She shook her head again. Derrington shuffled through his songs.

"Chris Brown?" he hoped.

"Nope." Dylan sighed, wondering if Massie kept boy music on her iPod for moments like these.

"What about Jonas Brothers?" Dylan squeezed her eyes shut, afraid of his reaction.

Derrington turned red. "Uh, whabum?"

"*What*?" Dylan giggled.

He inched closer, then mumbled, "What album?"

Dylan smiled. "*A Little Bit Longer*."

He thumb-spun the dial, then pressed. "Tell anyone I have this and you're more busted than my ankle."

"Pinky-swear." Dylan held out her pinky and he reached for it with his. They shook once but held on a half-second longer than friends usually did.

Derrington handed her a soap-filled bucket. "Cue up to 'BB Good,' and when I say go, hit play. If we each do two cars per song, we should be done in an hour."

Dylan's stomach base-jumped. Why did he want to be done so quickly? Wasn't he having fun? Didn't he like her? If Massie were there, would he want to be done in an hour?

"Ready?" he asked, oblivious to her inner turmoil. "One . . . two . . . threeeeeeee . . . Go!"

Dylan pressed play. The song started and they began bobbing their heads at the same time. Derrington got right to work.

He lifted the nubby pink sponge out of the bucket with zero regard for the dripping sudsy water or what it might do to his hands. Then he slapped it down on a black Jeep Liberty and began scrubbing.

Ehmagawd! He knew how to wash a car. And more than that, he didn't seem to think anything was wrong with that. It was blue-collar hawt.

Inspired, Dylan dunked her sponge with the same certainty.

Side by side they scrubbed, bobbing their heads and stealing occasional glances at each other. Whenever Derrington looked at Dylan, she'd smile serenely, like washing cars was her yoga. And whenever she looked at him, he scrubbed harder.

Ehma-shocking! Dylan thought, making soap hearts with her sponge. There she was doing manual labor and loving it. What next? A craving for beef jerky? The urge to shoot hoops after school? A belly shirt? How could a mere mortal trick her brain into thinking this was fun? Did Tom Cruise have that bewitching effect on Katie Holmes? Was that why she wore her hair like that?

Suddenly, an earthquake-size realization rattled Dylan. She and Derrington were soul mates! It was so ah-bvious. They had the same sense of humor. The same fair skin. The same ability to burp words. She recalled the days she and Kristen had fought over him. And how Massie settled the dispute by taking him for herself.

From then on, Dylan had hid her feelings like a skid-marked thong. Because coveting an alpha's crush was unethical. And *competing* with an alpha? Well, that was impossible. Besides, wasn't going from Massie to Dylan the same as switching from Gucci to Gap? George Clooney to George Bush? DSL to dial-up?

Dylan dipped her sponge and slapped it on a soiled white Acura. This time, the soap spilled down the hood like tears . . .

Ehmagawd! It was a sign! The universe was urging her to stop crushing on uncrushables. And if she didn't, she would ooze and gush and leak like a fat sponge. Just like she had when Massie had love-napped Derrington. Just like she had when Kemp and Plovert had ditched her because she'd overburped. Just like she had in Hawaii when J.T. had chosen Svetlana.

Well, those days were over, starting . . . NOW. No more reaching for the stars. From this moment on, Dylan would happily remain the kind of girl guys liked as friends. The girlfriend's girlfriend. The sad clown. She would never get hurt or embarrassed again. What was that expression? Once bitten twice shy?

Once bit-ten twice shy. Once bit-ten twice shy. Once bit-ten twice shy . . .

For the next twenty minutes, Dylan scrubbed the same spot to the rhythm of her new mantra.

Once bit-ten twice shy. Once bit-ten twice shy. Once bit-ten twice shy . . .

Her trance was interrupted by a text message sent from five cars away.

Derrington: U R a girl, right?

Dylan bit her bottom lip, hating herself for not glossing. Hating herself for not wearing prettier clothes. Hating herself for not being the kind of girl who normally thought washing cars was fun.

Dylan: Looking for proof? Cuz u can forget it.
Derrington: LOL! ☺

Dylan casually pulled a white earbud out of her ear and listened. He really was laughing out loud.

Once bit-ten twice whatever! Since when was she the shy type? Yes, she was funny, but not *every* guy saw that as a threat. And since they were soul mates, he ah-bviously appreciated her—

Derrington sent another text.

Derrington: U know what a 16-yr-old grl would want 4 her bday?

Dylan's chest deflated like a popped water bra. Of course he had a girlfriend. He just wanted to be friends. Same story, different outfit. Who was she kidding thinking that an alpha-dater would ever in a million years like a—

Derrington: Hu-llo? Answer pls.

Oops. What was the question? Dylan quickly scanned the conversation bubbles on her screen and then forced a convincing sad-clown smile.

Dylan: Easy. A 16-yr-old grl wants an 18-yr-old boy. ☺

Ha! Let him think I'm racy and experienced too.

She peeked at him through the side of her dVbs. He was laugh-typing.

Derrington: Ew! Not 4 my sister!!!

Dylan exhaled. She had to have more faith. According to Massie—or was it *Family Feud*—after "funny," the number two thing that turned boys off was "insecurity."

Dylan: Massie never told me u have a sister.
Derrington: There are a lot of things Massie doesn't know.
Dylan: Like ???
Derrington: My name is Derrick. Not Derrington. I wore shorts last winter cuz I lost a bet. I think red hair is cool.

Dylan lifted her eyes, silently asking the universe if maybe it had sent the wrong message. Maybe the suds had been a *good* sign. Representing a clean fresh start, not tears.

Derrington: So will you b-day shop with me tomorrow after doodie duty?
Dylan: Given. ☺

She dunked her sponge, squeezed out the excess water, and happily moved on to another car. But the more she scoured, the more insecurity frothed and foamed inside her brain like an overloaded bubble bath. Had Derrington asked her to shop because he wanted to hang, or because he wanted to make Massie jealous?

The more Dylan scrubbed, the more these doubts bubbled, until they spilled from her eyes and tasted like salt. Was this pendulum swing of emotion a normal by-product of meeting one's soul mate? Or was it her gut instinct, warning her not to get her hopes up? Fool in love, or just a fool? The facts were in, but the jury was out.

After waiting in the lobby for fourteen minutes, Kristen began climbing the two hundred and ten steps to her apartment, wondering the whole time if her mother had spite-stalled the elevator because she'd found out her daughter was showing leg.

Once her horror-film panting downgraded to human breathing, Kristen exited the stairwell and scanned the dimly lit hall for signs of her mom's early arrival, keeping an eye out for giveaways like:

A) White nurse shoes on the teak welcome mat.
B) A forgotten grocery bag dangling from the doorknob.
C) David Beckham running loose in the hall.
D) The smell of tomato sauce and/or fabric softener.

Thankfully, Kristen noted none of the above. Apartment 10F and its perimeter were secure. The only things that stood out were the new neighbor's creepy totem pole and the team of First Rate Movers who were force-jamming it into the narrow entryway. Then she saw the *elevator*. It was stuffed with boxes and propped open by an elephant-tusk coffee table.

Kristen turned her key with silent precision. She vowed that if she made it across the parquet floor to her bedroom undetected, she'd never risk wearing her Range Rover–replaced outfit home again.

Marsha Purdy Gregory + plaid short shorts + a gray V-neck bell-sleeve sweater + knee-high black moccasins = being forced to don a burka until college graduation.

"Heeeey, Beckham," Kristen whisper-squealed when she saw the fluffy white Persian curled on her twin bed like a croissant. The kitty lifted his head, but Kristen denied him love until her knee-length sweat shorts and loose matching gray T-shirt were on and her illegal fly-arrhea-stained outfit was gone.

"Safe!" She fell back on her blue and green polka-dot duvet and spoon-hugged Beckham. Then she tried to imagine the Pretty Committee hanging in her bedroom.

The lime green bedside lamp was the same lime as the beanbag, which was the same lime as the polka dots on her duvet, which were the same lime as the walls. The room was so thoroughly coordinated she could probably convince them that someone other than the online shopping assistant at potterybarn.com had decorated it.

"Not that I'd ever have the chance." Kristen sighed aloud. "We're ah-bviously not good enough for them." She squeezed Beckham's warm belly and buried her face in his fur. He smelled like coconut shampoo, a little something she'd invested in to remind them of Dune.

"Seven more sleeps and he'll be back."

Beckham sighed.

Kristen rolled onto her back and blew a kiss at the photo of Dune Baxter taped to her ceiling. The sun was setting behind him, drenching the background in golden light that matched his skin. He was lying on a longboard, brown eyes staring straight into the camera, his smile relaxed yet stoked. For a moment, Kristen could smell his tropical fruit–scented sunscreen.

Dune grinned back, like he was thanking her for being smart enough to have scored a summer job tutoring his younger sister, Ripple, so they could meet and become C-pluses. Well, at least that's what she *liked* to believe his grin was saying.

"You're welcome," Kristen mouthed back. "Thanks for being a CLAM," she whispered to her cute, loyal, athletic, middle-class crush.

"*He* likes coming over," she mumbled in Beckham's triangular ear. "*He's* not a snob like certain OCDivas we know," she said, recalling Dune's nickname for the Pretty Committee. Her insides warmed just using his term. It made her feel closer to him, like he wasn't surf-modeling on some heart-shaped, impossible-to-get-cell-service-on island in the South Pacific, but right there beside her.

A startling crash, immediately followed by a muffled shouting match between an angry woman and an apologetic Russian First Rate Mover, came from next door.

"Reeee-ow!" Beckham bolted under the bed.

Kristen buried her face in a pillow. "Thank Gawd," she mumbled, suddenly relieved that Massie had turned down her *après*-school invitation after all. Thin was in when it came to waists, nawt walls.

Her black Razr rang "Need U Bad" by Jazmine Sullivan—something it only did in extreme emergencies.

Boy I need U bad as my heartbeat,
Bad like the food I eat . . .

Kristen shot up and speed-answered. "Why aren't you using the WCC?" she whisper-hissed. "What if Massie was here? What if we got caught?"

"Relax," the girl on the other end whisper-hissed back. "This isn't official Witty Committee business, so I didn't want to use the Witty Committee computer. It's an abuse of power."

Kristen rolled her eyes. She was just as serious as Layne about their secret underground society of five, who paid homage to their favorite historical Gifted people by dressing up as them and meeting online to discuss all things intellectual. But if Massie ever found out Kristen was:

A) Cleopatra!
B) Friends with LBR Layne Abeley, who dressed up as Albert Einstein.
C) Friends with LBR Rachel Walker, who dressed up as Oprah.
D) Friends with LBR Aimee Snyder, who dressed up as Shakespeare.
E) Friends with LBR Danh Bondok, who dressed up as Bill Gates (and who Massie called Candy Corn).
F) All of the above. ✓

Massie would cover her in meat-flavored Glossip Girl and feed her to Bean.

"We need to talk," Layne insisted. "Not Einstein and Cleopatra. As *us*."

"But—"

"Butts are for sitting!" Layne interrupted. "School has been in session for weeks, and I haven't made any progress with *Dempsey*." She whispered her lifelong crush's name like he was a wanted criminal. "None. I thought the *Wizard of Claus* callbacks would be my chance for romance, but Massie was there and completely Block-blocked me!"

"What? Why was *she* there?" Kristen's forehead barfed sweat. Her best friend and her secret best friend were crushing on the same boy. Her two worlds were hurtling toward each other like Heidi and L.C., doomed to collide. "She wasn't *auditioning*, was she?"

"No, Joe, she was giving Dempsey *acting* advice," Layne scoffed.

"How does she know—"

"She said she learned a lot on the set of *Dial L for Loser*. Can you believe it?"

"Yep." Kristen nodded as if Layne could actually see her. When Massie Block wanted something, the truth was a ball and she could bend it like Beckham (the soccer player, not the cat).

"Wanna see?" There were a few beeps and then: "Check out the video."

A quaking shot of Massie and Dempsey's backs filled the Razr's tiny screen. They were seated in the rear of the auditorium giggling at some guy's off-key rendition of "Happy Birthday."

"Zero presence," she could hear Massie mutter. "Zero connection with the audience. *Zee*-ro! I don't believe he's really wishing someone a happy birthday. I don't believe he *cares*."

"Yeah, I totally see that." Dempsey nodded.

"You need to cuh-nect," Massie insisted, "or you'll never make it in this business."

The video ended abruptly.

"She doesn't like him, does she?" Layne squeaked. "Because if she does, you *have* to break them apart. You promised me. I helped you get Skye Hamilton away from Dune this summer, and you promised you'd help me get Dempsey. Remember?"

Kristen bit her throbbing hangnail.

"Re-mem-ber?"

Of course she remembered. That was why she'd spent all morning trying to convince Massie that her new crush was an LBR.

Kristen paced across her green shag rug. The fibers that usually tickled her feet seemed unusually coarse.

"Reeeee-meeeemmmmm-berrrrrrrr?"

She stomped her foot.

"Yes. Yes, I remember, okay? But it's not that easy."

"Neither was breaking into the country club, filling the pool with Jell-O, creating a video reflection so it looked like water, and timing it so that Skye jumped in before Dune. But I did it. And now if you'd kindly place your hand on your neck and feel the shark tooth, I think you'll agree that the plan worked and—"

"Okay, okay! What do you want me to do?"

"Find out if he likes me," Layne cooed sweetly. "And if he says no, then *make* him change his mind."

Kristen's ears began to ring. It was hell calling.

"Layne, I totally want to help, but I hardly even know the guy," she tried. "Can't you just have an honest conversation with Dempsey? You've been opposite-sex best friends for years."

"We *were* opposite-sex best friends." Layne sighed. "Now that I like him, I can't talk to him anymore. I'm too—"

"Hold on," Kristen interrupted. "What, Mom?" she called into her empty apartment. "I'm on the phone!" She paused like she was listening to her mother. But the only shouting woman she could actually hear was the new stressed-out neighbor next door. "*Okay*! Stop yelling. I'll be right there." After an extra-long sigh Kristen moaned, "I gotta go."

"No prob, slob," Layne replied. "Looking forward to the good word, yellow bird. I'll check in tomorrow."

The line went dead.

With shaking hands, Kristen reached under the bed and grabbed her soccer ball—the only thing she could kick repeatedly without being arrested.

The rooftop of the Pinewood was paved with uneven bricks, cigarette butts, and flattened beer cans. But it had a tall concrete wall around its perimeter that overlooked the building's grassy courtyard and could sustain the force of a stress-kicked soccer ball. It was Kristen's go-to place when things got complicated, like Massie had Bean . . . Alicia had her dance studio . . . Claire had her fingernails . . . and Dylan had her fridge. And things *were* complicated.

Kick!

The ball slammed against the concrete wall and shot back to her. She kicked it again.

Slam!

She'd *promised* Layne she'd help her get Dempsey. They'd made a deal.

Slam!

If she reneged, she would destroy her good name and honor in the eyes of the Witty Committee.

Slam!

But how could she sabotage Massie's new crush? She had made a pledge. She had taken a vow. *This time we'll do it right. . . . Our friendships come first. . . . PC support, day or night . . . Or that member will be cursed. CURSED!*

Kick!

Slam!

Kick!

It was a lose-lose situation. And the only neutral person she could turn to for advice was surfing on a heart-shaped island with no cell service.

Kick!

Kick!

Kick!

Like a loyal dog, the ball landed at her turquoise and white Adidas cleats. Kristen stepped on it and lifted her gaze.

A sudden gust of wind broke a solid mass of gray clouds into a smiley face that seemed to say, *Let the Big Guy help.*

Swept up in a rush of divine inspiration, she began gathering beer cans. Once her hands were full she built two towers, paying little mind to the burp-scented liquid that dribbled down her wrist while she stacked.

"Okay." She sighed aloud. "If I hit the one on the right, you want me to help Massie. If I hit the one on the left, you want me to help Layne." Kristen glanced up at the smiley cloud, making sure it was still watching. "Ready?"

She spun three times, squeezed her lids shut, and kicked!

On the street below, the brakes on a passing truck wheezed to a stop. A dog barked. Two little boys giggle-ran through the courtyard. But no cans crashed to the ground. And no ball slammed against the concrete wall.

Kristen opened her eyes.

And then she blushed.

Dempsey Solomon appeared in front of her wearing mir-rored aviators, spinning the soccer ball between his two index fingers, and grinning.

"What're you doing here?" she asked, feeling slightly em-barrassed. Like that time she had a lip-kiss dream about Danh and then saw him the next morning.

"I'll tell you if you can go *around the world*."

Demonstrating, he kicked the ball from his right foot to his thigh to his shoulder to his head to his left shoulder to his left thigh to his left foot to Kristen.

"Done." She stopped the ball with her heel and then took it where it needed to go.

When she was done, Kristen giggled for a second longer than normal, while her mind recalibrated and reevaluated all previous notions of Dempsey. He was more than just a wannabe actor who'd lost weight over the summer, invested in contacts, tanned evenly, dressed like a rugged safari guide, and steeped himself in African culture, thereby enriching his soul and broadening his global perspective—he was soccer-licious! Kristen could now see why Massie and Layne had picked him as their C-plus.

"Where did you learn that?" Kristen blurted. "I always thought you were—" She paused, not wanting to insult him, but also not knowing what to say.

"A couch potato theater dork?" he finished for her.

Kristen blushed again.

"I was." His confident smile told her that he was okay

with that. "I mean, I'm still into theater. But I'm also super into *football*."

Kristen twirled her shark-tooth necklace, oddly charmed by his use of the British term, something she usually found beyond pretentious. "Since *when*?"

"Since Africa." He tugged the zipper on his olive green hoodie. "My family volunteered at an orphanage in Tanzania, and the older kids taught my brother and I how to play."

My brother and me, Kristen thought with some relief. Her mom had warned her about boys who were too perfect: They were not to be trusted. And until this minor grammatical infraction, his picture had been on all twelve pages of the "too perfect" calendar.

"So what *are* you doing here, anyway?" She bounced the ball on her knee. Dempsey caught it with his foot, knocked it to his head, and shot it forward like a dolphin at SeaWorld.

Both beer towers crashed to the ground. "I'm your new neighbor."

"Seriously?" she gasped.

"Yeah. After living in African mud huts, my parents walked into our house on Tuxedo Way and thought it was too much. So they sold it and bought something cozier." He stuffed his hands in the pockets of his worn khaki cargos. "And sent the leftover money to them." He pointed east.

Kristen grin-nodded like she was warmed by their generous decision, not offended that her home had been compared to an African mud hut.

"So we've been moving in all day, and everything was

going fine until the red river-clay dishes broke," Dempsey continued. "And my mom started freaking out. And the apartment started feeling really small and cramped. So I came up here." He shrugged. "Africa is so big and open. And ever since I got back, I've felt trapped, you know? Like everything is closing in on me. And all I want to do is be free."

The image of Layne and Massie on either side of Dempsey, crushing their crush into a panini, gave Kristen pause. Maybe, out of respect for his claustrophobia, it would be best to give him some space. And then, once he acclimated, she could talk to him about the *Lassie* situation.

Satisfied, Kristen kicked the ball. The instant it bounced back, Dempsey toe-lifted it onto his knee and took it around the world again.

Gawd, couldn't he miss once?

"We're back!" Massie bit into a crisp organic carrot and settled into the bamboo chair at the head of number eighteen.

"We're back!" The Pretty Committee rose out of their seats, lifted their farm-fresh vegetables, and clinked them together like champagne flutes.

The New Green Café, which had been transformed into a sun-soaked greenhouse over the summer, was teeming with lunching coeds. They all stole glances at the Pretty Committee over plates of fresh produce and frothing glasses of skin-purifying Borba juice.

"Our days of eating low-fat turkey Subway sandwiches in the overflow trailers are over." Massie unscrewed the top off a bottle of Rodeo Drive, Chanel's latest purple polish. "Time to mark our territory." She crouched down and began painting *BFFWC* under the bamboo table. And then she spotted the happy little pen hearts Claire had drawn on the rubber toe of her red Converse and gagged carrot.

What was it about friends in love that made them so annoying?

"Hey there." A familiar pair of scuffed-up Timberlands stopped at their table. "What's up, neighbor?"

Neighbor?

Massie suddenly forgot all about Claire's hearts. Her own was much more important.

"Neighborrrrrrrrr," Dylan burped.

"Ewwww." Kristen giggle-waved the air. "Egg!"

"Egg *whites*," Dylan proudly corrected.

"Dempsey." Massie ran her fingers over her low side-pony and stood with a smile.

He smiled back, his worn white crewneck accentuating his Tanzania tan. He rested his hand on the back of Kristen's chair.

"You're moving to table seventeen?" Massie looked left, wondering why he or anyone else would ever want to sit with BOGUSS (Briarwood-Octavian Government Unification Students' Society). The table was permanently empty. They didn't even want to sit with themselves.

"No." Dempsey snickered, his dimples carving mini-smiles in his cheeks. "I mean me and Kristen are neighbors."

Kristen and I, Massie thought, but didn't bother correcting him. He had just come from Africa and was probably still readjusting to the language.

And then it hit her.

"Neighbors?" she squealed. "As in, you live in an *apartment*?"

"Yeah." He beamed. "It's cozy. I like it."

Massie purposely ignored Kristen's triumphant grin.

"EhMa-*cute!*" She smoothed the brown faux fur on her Juicy swing coat and *why-didn't-you-tell-me-that?* glared at Kristen. "I ah-dore the Pinewood."

Kristen fake-coughed.

Massie snatched Dylan's bag of blue chips. "Terra?"

"Hey—" Dylan started to protest. But Massie silenced her with an elbow to the spine.

"Thanks." Dempsey dug in and poked around for just the right chip. Clearly they were perfect for each other. If she ate chips, she would have done the exact same thing.

"Ever tried the spicy ones?" Layne suddenly appeared out of nowhere and thrust a black bag under his chin.

"Hey, Mrs. Claus." Dempsey liberated his hand from Massie's bag and put it in Layne's.

"Don't jinx me." Layne lifted the gray feather–covered fedora off her head and fanned her flushed visage like a 1940s film star. "They haven't made the announcement yet."

"Has anyone announced that you're stealing diseased pigeon feathers and gluing them to your fedor-ka?" Massie inquired.

"Yeah. *Teen Vogue* is writing about it in next month's DIY section." Layne proudly stuck the hat back on her head.

"Disease-Infected Youth?" Massie lifted her high-five hand. But for some reason Dylan was the only one who giggle-smacked it. Dempsey didn't smile. Obviously, he was trying to be nice to the LBR because they were pre-makeover friends. And like any decent human being, he planned to wait the recommended twelve weeks before dumping her. By Thanksgiving, Layne would be outed like Clay Aiken on the 9/27/08 cover of *People* magazine.

"What's up?" Derrington called, limping toward their table. He was wearing a bright green BOCD Golf visor, the matching jacket, and madras pants. Massie fought the urge to call him Tiger, because he'd assume she was flirting. And why lead him on?

"What are you *wearing*?" Dylan fluffed her red hair.

Derrington took a massive bite of tofu dog. "Josh Bankman's golf uniform." He chewed, and then polished off the rest of the dog. "I had to sneak into the café. I can't eat in those trailers." He dumped a paper cone filled with sweet-potato fry crumbs in his mouth. "They smell like pickles."

He reached into his plaid pocket and pulled out a bag of sours. "Here." He tossed them at Claire. "From Cam."

"Awwww." Claire's smile was so wide, she practically swallowed her own ears.

"So Splenda!" Massie cooed, pretending to be moved by the sickly sweet gesture, even though she was really sending a subliminal message to Dempsey that said, *If you ever did something like that for me, I would react favorably.*

Derrington flicked Layne on the padded shoulder of her secondhand history teacher tweed blazer.

"Owie!" She flicked him back.

"How did *you* get in here? You're supposed to be in the trailers too."

Layne unfolded a note written on school letterhead. "Principal Burns gave me permission because Alicia's going to announce the cast of *The Wizard of Claus*, and I auditioned for the lead and—"

"Does anyone have any ice?" Derrington cut her off. "My foot is swelling."

"Lemme see." Dylan beamed.

Derrington grabbed his plaid pants at the knee and lifted his leg. "Whoa." He teetered left. Then right. Then left. Then he fell on his butt by Massie's gray suede ankle boots. "Ahhhhh!" He rocked back and forth.

Massie rolled her eyes and stepped away from the spectacle. *Gawd, would he stop at nothing to get her attention?*

"Ehmagawd." Dylan raced to his side. "Y'okay?"

"Yeah," he moaned while she helped him onto her chair. "I went to soccer practice and tried to push through the pain. And it got worse." Derrington lifted his leg and pulled off his white sweat sock to reveal a black and blue foot the size of a walrus flipper.

Claire pity-gasped. Massie turned away in disgust.

"Now I'm off the team until it gets better." He smiled like someone who had better things to do, even though he probably didn't. "Looks like I'll have a lot of free time after school now."

"Well, I won't," Massie blurted, just to be clear. "I'm getting involved in the arts," she said loud enough for Dempsey to hear.

"But you're the best player on the team," Kristen whined. "And now that we're one school, the Tomahawks' score affects our overall standing. You could totally bring down the Sirens."

"Thanks for caring," Derrington teased his fellow captain, wincing in pain.

"Good afternoon." Alicia's voice crackled from the speakers. "This is Alicia Rivera with your lunchtime news brief."

Everyone in the café took their seats and stopped talking—not because they cared about school news, but because they thought she was hot.

"First up, the Christmas play."

Layne squeezed Dempsey's arm. Massie flicked a soybean at her back.

"I am pleased to announce that this year's female and male lead in *The Wizard of Claus* will be played by Layne Abeley and Dempsey Solomon."

"YESSSSSS!" Layne threw her fedora in the air. A flurry of mangy pigeon feathers drifted to the ground.

Dempsey threw his tanned arms around her and lifted her into the air. Massie flicked another soybean, this time pegging Layne on the cheek.

Dylan threw her head back and cracked up.

"Jealous much?" Layne shouted at the entire café, having no idea who the soy-shooter was.

Massie summoned Layne to the head of the table with an index finger. "Hey," she whispered, "where did she say those rehearsals were?"

Layne exhaled sharply, poisoning Massie's air with spicy chip smell. "Don't even *think* of stealing the female lead. It's already mine."

"Puh-lease!" Massie slapped her heart. "I wouldn't dream of it."

Layne leaned in a little closer. "Then what do you want?"

"The *male* lead." Massie winked. Then, just to be perfectly clear, she pulled out a travel-size bottle of Chanel No. 19, leaned forward, and spritzed the back of Dempsey's olive green hoodie three times.

Derrington waved the iris-scented air. "Dude, is that you?"

Dempsey sniffed the back of his sweatshirt with marked concern.

"Don't worry," Derrington assured him. "The same thing happened to me a few months ago. I think it means you've been touched by an angel."

"More like the devil," Layne mumbled. Her phone beeped with a text.

Massie: I marked him. He's mine. ☺

Layne's thick eyebrows collided. "You can't do that!"

"What?" Dylan asked, peeking at Layne's screen. And then immediately began typing.

Dylan: U marked Derrington and now you're over him. U sure u mean it this time? Isn't marking forever?

Massie glowered across the table before responding. Why was everyone being so negative lately?

Massie: I can un-mark him by soaking him with water.
Dylan: U going to unmark Derrington?
Massie: Some day.
Dylan: U don't even like him anymore.
Massie: Doesn't mean he can like someone else.

"But—" Dylan tried, looking up from her iPhone.

"Butts are for toning," Massie snapped, resenting the sudden challenge. Not only was it undermining, it was taking her attention away from Dempsey. And if she didn't keep him occupied, he might leave. "Now shhhhhh." She pointed at the speaker on the ceiling, then lifted her finger to her lips.

". . . The rest of the cast list will be posted outside the auditorium after lunch," Alicia continued. "Now on to sports. Tomahawks captain Derringt—I mean, Derrick Harrington—" She giggled. "—injured his foot in an unfortunate incident that involved a tree and gravity. He's been benched until he's made a full recovery. Soccer tryouts to fill his position will take place Friday after school. Now on to parents night . . ."

"Dempsey!" Kristen turned around and blurt-smacked his hand. "You should totally do it."

"Me?" Dempsey chuckled.

"Him?" Massie leaned forward, smacked the table, and gasped.

Kristen leaned toward her. "He's ah-mazing," she explained. "I saw him play last night and—"

"I was just messing around. I can't—"

"That's right—he *can't*." Layne nudged Kristen. "Rehearsals for *Wizard of Claus* start tonight. Re-mem-beeeer?"

"Yeah, but he's really good and our school needs—"

"But Dempsey's not into soccer," Massie insisted. "And we're over watching soccer games after school, re-mem-ber? We're into the arts." She looked beside her, hoping Claire might back her up, but she was giggle-texting Cam, which was even more annoying than this conversation.

"Dude, if you're that good, maybe you *should* try out." Derrington adjusted the green brim on his visor. "Maybe that's what the angel's try'na tell you."

"Ya think?" Dempsey cocked his head, considering this.

"What about the play?" Layne whined.

"It's not like I'm going to make it," he assured her. "I'm just gonna try out. You know, for fun."

"But you *will* make it." Kristen's pale cheeks were flushed with excitement. "I know it."

"If you're that good, you *have* to do it," Derrington urged. "The team needs you."

"Okay." Dempsey shrugged. "I guess I could try soccer for a few weeks. To honor the African orphans." He beamed.

"Madonna will be so proud," Dylan blurted from across the table.

"Seriously?" Layne stomped her metallic gold Converse high-top. "You're quitting the show?"

"Why not?" Dempsey shrugged. "I'll do the play next semester."

"Sellout!" Layne crumpled up her chip bag, whipped it at his neck, then took off in a huff, bashing into unsuspecting students as she zigzagged through the maze of bamboo tables.

"Wait!" Dempsey called after her.

"Don't let her bring you down." Massie stood and placed a reassuring hand on his shoulder. "This new opportunity is too exciting."

Claire finally stopped texting. "I thought you hated soccer?"

"Me?" Massie gripped her heart in shock and fell back into her chair at the head of the table, like someone close to fainting. "Puh-lease! I toe-da-lly support sports." She beamed invisible "shut up" rays from her eyes. *Gawd!* Claire of all people should have understood the sacrifices one must make for love. She rode to school every day on Cam's bike! She had given up heated leather luxury SUV seats for the back half of a hard triangular stump.

"You *do*?" Kristen pushed her plate of sweet-potato fries aside. "How?"

Dylan reached over and helped herself to a handful. Derrington, who was now standing behind her, grabbed them out of her hand and stuffed them in his own mouth. Dylan giggled, reaching for more.

"Whaddaya mean *how*?" Massie's cheeks reddened. "My, you know, dream of starting a cheerleading squad."

Claire burst out laughing.

"What?" Massie leaned to the right and smacked Claire's thigh when Dempsey wasn't looking.

"Seriously?" Kristen cackled. "Cheerleading for *soccer*?"

"Why nawt?" Dylan chewed. "You know how many calories we'll burn?"

"I say we have our first meeting Friday night," Massie announced. "At Kristen's house."

"I thought it was a *condo*." Kristen shot her a side glance.

Massie pouted in an "I feel sad for you right now" sort of

way. "K, why are you always putting your cute little apartment down? I think it's cozy."

"That's what *I* think." Dempsey leaned across the table and high-fived Massie. A fiery-hot crush-bolt shot up her arm the instant they made contact.

"Ehmagawd, that's right! You live there. I totally forgot." Kristen rolled her eyes.

Claire smile-bit her pinky nail, half listening and half texting Cam.

"Maybe we'll run into you Friday night."

"May-*be*." Dempsey nodded back.

Massie beamed. *Gimme a YAY!*

CURRENT STATE OF THE UNION

IN	OUT
The Pinewood Building	The Block Estate
Cleats	Claus
Cheering coach	Acting coach

Dylan had imagined herself riding doubles on the back of a boy's bike many times before. A silk Hermès scarf tied around her red curls . . . tanned calves glistening in the sunlight . . . cashmere-coated arms hugging a distressed leather jacket . . . But never had she envisioned herself post-detention, wearing pigeon poo–covered sweats, red rain boots, and gripping a hoodie with cracked dishpan hands. Yet there she was, on Derrington's silver BMX, off to buy his sister a birthday present. And she had never felt more beautiful.

Students lumbering home under the weight of their backpacks envy-glanced as they passed. Dylan made sure they saw her "my life is so perfect I'm bored" expression. Lids heavy . . . mouth relaxed . . . hungry.

After a few blocks, Derrington started to slow down. And then the bike started to wobble.

Am I too fat?

Dylan spit out her wad of Twisted Tornado Bubblicious, hoping to lighten the load. Still, the bike swayed from side to side.

"I should get off," Dylan managed, despite the lump in her throat.

"Good idea." Derrington slammed on the brakes.

"What?"

"My ankle." He began loosening his laces.

"Oh!" The throat lump disintegrated. "Want me to pedal?"

He folded his arms across his chest and shrugged.

"Trade places," Dylan insisted, feeling revitalized and fabulously in control. She straddled the banana seat and honked his horn. "Clear the road!"

She sucked in her abs when he gripped her waist and managed to hold them in as she power-pedaled for the next eight blocks.

Rosemary mint shampoo wafted off Dylan's hair and enveloped them in what she pictured to be an invisible scented heart. . . . Then a vision of Massie formed in her head, or rather, what the alpha would do if she saw them right now. And the heart scattered like glitter in the wind.

"You're strong," Derrington mused, thumb-drumming on her back as they rounded the corner onto Main Street.

OMG, he thinks I'm a man. Massie would never pedal a boy. Not even for charity!

"He's injured, *okay*?" Dylan shouted at a gawking toddler in a pink fleece–lined stroller.

Derrington leaned forward and honked his horn as they weaved through the foot traffic.

Beep beep beep beeeeeeeeeeeeeeep. Beep beep beep beep beeeeeeeep. Beep beep beep beeeeeeeeeeeeeeep. Beep beep beep beep beeeeeeeep.

They cut through the middle of the sidewalk, forcing pedestrians to pick a side or perish. Shopping bags, children, and teacup dogs were yanked out of harm's way with such urgency Dylan couldn't stop pedal-laughing. Or was the giddiness a side effect directly related to Derrington's chest being pressed up against her back? Either way, she needed to get off the black bike and show this boy that despite her strong legs and extreme mouth gas, she was all lady. And she would start by calling him *Derrick*.

"Here we are, *Derrick*." She hit the brakes in front of Amazing Lace, a small boutique with big prices. "Shall we go in, *Derrick*?"

Saying his real name gave her that awkward French-class feeling. Like when Madame Vallon made her speak with the correct accent—*It's not jam-bone; it's jahhhhhm-bon!* It sounded forced and unnatural coming from her mouth. But Dylan wanted *Derrick* to know that, unlike Massie, *she* respected him. At the very least it might make up for her manly strength.

Derrington straddle-backed off the bike with the grace of someone who peed his pants. He limped over to the store window.

"What is this place?" he asked, pig-pressing his nose to the glass and fogging it up. Then he winked at the mannequin. "Hey, hottie."

OMG, does he think she's cuter than me? Is it her feminine dress? Her fat-free body? Her hard plaster stomach? Her pointy braless—

"Are you sure this place is right for my sister?" he asked, a look of concern in his eyes.

Truth be told, Dylan had no clue whether this store was

right for his sister. Until yesterday, she hadn't even known he had a sister. But she *did* know their dresses were imported. And that meant their sizing was all over the place. Sixes were often fours, fours were twos, and twos were zeros. What better way to remind him that she was a girl than to try on frilly outfits in petite sizes?

"I think your sister will love their stuff. Why don't I try a few things on so you can see how they look?" Dylan held the door open and Derrington limped in.

Hold awn! Wasn't the girl supposed to wait for the boy to open the door? Or were the rules different if the boy was injured?

It was funny. The person she wanted to ask was the same person she was hoping to avoid. She'd always gone to Massie with her crush questions, but clearly that was no longer an option.

The smell of soap and candles soothed Dylan instantly. "Is Katya here?" she asked the posture-perfect blonde dusting the glass jewelry display case.

"Vacation." The woman lowered her head and peered out over her glasses. "My name is Camille. Camille Onuoha. Can I hulp you?" she asked like someone swallowing a pill without water.

"Just looking." Dylan bit her lip, trying not to laugh at her accent.

"Gross!" Derrington pushed a bowl of potpourri aside and then promptly sneezed. Dozens of dried flower buds blew to the floor. "That smelled exactly like Principal Burns."

"Ew!" Dylan burst out laughing.

"Lets get outta here." Derrington smashed into a table of silk scarves on his way to the exit.

"Wait!" Dylan's smile faded quickly. "I'm just gonna grab a few size-*four* dresses and slip them on. You know, to help you get an idea of what your sister will like."

"The only thing you're *grabbing* is that potpourri." Camille pinched the bowl and marched it over to the register. "*If* you can afford it."

Dylan's heart began to pound. Had she not been humiliated enough for one day? Pigeon poo–covered sweats? Biking a boy though town? And now mistaken for a vagrant?

"How much is it?" Derrington pulled a crumpled twenty out of his jeans. "I guess my sister could use it in her bathroom." He fanned the air in front of his nose. "She's a total bran lover."

Dylan cracked up.

"It's *sixty* dollars." The woman scowled, folding her thin arms across her flat chest. "You need forty more."

"I got it." Dylan slapped down her ultra-exclusive American Express black card.

Camille lifted the card to her face. "You are *hardly* Merri-Lee Marvil." She reached for the phone.

"True." Dylan grinned. "But my *mother* is."

"Score!" Derrington wiggled his butt.

"I'm so sorry, Ms. Marvil." The woman managed a smile as she put the phone back down. "It's just, with credit card fraud being what it is . . ." Her voice trailed off for a moment.

"Let me help you start a room. We have some lovely things from Brazil. And of course we can forget about the potpourri mishap."

"Maybe *you* can"—Dylan fake-sniffled—"but I can't. And neither will my mother."

"But—"

"Butts are for kissing!" Dylan shouted back. "So kiss this!" She wiggled her rear while Derrington stuck the mannequin's bony fingers up her perfect mannequin nose. And with a flip of her rosemary-mint scented hair, Dylan marched out.

They laughed all the way to the dollar store. They laughed while they picked out sixteen "sweet" presents for his sister— a massive jawbreaker, caramel-scented car-freshener, and earmuffs shaped like lambs. They laughed while he bought Pinkberry with the change. And they laughed while they shared it.

So what if her size-four fashion show never got off the ground? The rest of her was soaring.

"Come awn, Beckham, just wear it!" Kristen finally managed to slip the black satin bow tie over her cat's joggling head. "There." She collapsed onto her lime green beanbag after the eighteen-minute struggle. "You look ah-dorable. If cats could see their reflections, I'd show you. You'll just have to trust me."

The white Persian leapt up on the bed and burrowed under the green throw pillows.

"I know you're mad." Kristen raced to smooth the Beckham-shaped dent in her comforter. "But when everyone says how handsome you look, you'll thank me."

Beckham sneezed.

"This is the first time I've ever hosted a Friday night sleepover," Kristen tried. But the significance of this milestone was lost on the fluffy cat. "Don't you get it? This is the first time anyone's ever seen our room. The first time you're going to meet the Pretty Committee. Becks, you could be the new *Bean*!"

Beckham emerged cautiously. "That's better." Kristen kissed the top of his head, then ran through her checklist—*ah-gain*—to make sure her twenty-dollar catering budget (jeez, thanks, Mom ☹) read more like fifty.

64

FRIDAY NIGHT
SLEEPOVER CHECKLIST

1) Five red Crate and Barrel plates placed exactly three
   inches apart on my desk, just like at Massie's house.
   Each piled high with a different snack and labeled
   accordingly.

2) Edamame (frozen kind)

3) Hummus platter (hummus, pita, and four black olives
   left over from Mom's Wednesday night book club)

4) Sweet 'n' Salty Surprise (three Hershey's bars
   melted over two bags of Rold Golds from the vending
   machine near Mom's desk at Mercy Me—aka Mercy
   Memorial Hospital)

5) "Gourmet Italian popcorn" (Pop Secret doused in
   Kraft grated parmesan cheese)

6) Gummy in My Tummy (a sweaty heap of worms and
   feet from 7-Eleven)

7) Crème brûlée–scented room spray

8) Lavender-scented sheet spray (for sleeping bags—
   a stocking stuffer from Massie last Christmas)

9) SOS (Sleep Over Songs)

- "A Little Bit Longer" —Jonas Brothers
- "Tell Me Something I Don't Know" —Selena Gomez
- "Wake Up Call" —Hayden Panettiere
- "I'm Yours" —Jason Mraz
- "First Love" —Karina
- "One Love" —Jordan Pruitt
- "Footballer's Wife" —Amy MacDonald
- "Losing Grip" —Avril Lavigne
- "You Think" —Clique Girlz

"Heyyyyyy," a familiar voice bellowed from the hall-way.

Before Kristen could check the thermostat to confirm that the apartment was Massie-warm at a balmy seventy-six degrees, her bedroom door burst open.

Massie appeared, her amber eyes scanning the room like teeth on a corncob.

"I didn't even hear—"

"Your mom let us in," she offered, practically reading Kristen's mind. "Is it cold in here?" She shuddered.

"Opposite." Alicia rested her chin on Massie's shoulder

and fanned her flushed cheeks. "I think the *coziness* of this place makes it feel kind of warm. Don't you?"

"I like it." Claire poked her head out from behind Alicia. Her smile was genuine and helped Kristen relax . . . a little.

"Cozzzzzyyyyyyy," Dylan burped from the hallway. "Ugh, green pepper."

"Ewwww!" Everyone giggle-rushed into Kristen's bedroom to avoid the fumes.

So far so good. Kristen sighed happily. They were laughing. That meant they were having fun and making memories. And memories, when fermented, become inside jokes, which by the way are *the* highest form of flattery. Kristen could hear it all now. They'd be walking to class on Monday and Massie would say, "Remember Kristen's sleepover when Dylan burped and we all ran away from her green pepper breath?"

Everyone would lose themselves laughing and associate Kristen and her house with ah-mazing times. And this was just the beginning. The night had yet to realize its "ah-mazing time" potential. Dozens of inside jokes were out there, floating around, just waiting to be discovered.

"Snacks?" Kristen pressed play on her bedside iPod.

"Jonas Brothers!" Dylan clapped with unexpected delight.

The girls stepped onto the blue shag area rug and dropped their sleeping bags. Something about the way they looked in her room—cloaked in fine silk sleepwear (except Claire, who was in cotton thermals), their long layers held back with color-coordinated sleep masks—reminded Kristen of the time she'd visited her old kindergarten teacher. She had felt gigantic next to the mini-chairs and knee-high snack tables. Was that how the PC felt right now?

"This is Beckham." She scooped up her cat and swung him back and forth like he was on an invisible ship in a raging storm.

"I didn't know you had one of those." Massie hooked her black quilted Marc Jacobs tote over her shoulder, even though it was already hooked.

"What about all those pictures on my phone and in my wallet and in my binders and—"

"I thought they came with the frames." Massie adjusted her lilac *In Your Dreams* sleep mask.

"I always thought Beckham was your imaginary boyfriend." Alicia flopped down on Kristen's bed.

"Just like Josh is yours?" Dylan joked.

"Just like *no one* is yours?" Alicia raised her perfectly plucked eyebrows.

"Awwwwww, he's cute." Claire petted him. "Come feel how soft he is."

"He smells like coconuts." Kristen buried her nose in his white fur.

A low grumble came from Massie's black quilted Marc Jacobs tote. At first Kristen thought it was the alpha's stomach . . . until the grumble barked.

"Lady behavior, Bean!" Massie commanded. But the black pug, who was dressed in a moss green silk cami and boy shorts, ignored her. Instead she jumped out of the bag and leapt toward Beckham.

"Ahhhhhh!" Kristen shouted, startled by the sudden attack.

Beckham jumped out of Kristen's arms and landed feetfirst on the bed. Bean hopped up three times, trying to get up on the bed, while Beckham hiss-paced frantically.

Claire, Alicia, and Dylan clung to each other for safety.

"Awww, baby, want some help?" Massie cooed, then lifted Bean onto the bed.

The dog went straight for the cat's bow tie, clawing and growling at it as if it were a direct threat.

"Re-owwww!" Beckham sprang onto his hind legs and batted Bean's face like it was made of yarn.

Kristen scooped up her cat with urgency. "Why did you put her up there?" she screeched.

"Oops." Massie covered her mouth daintily, like a society girl with hiccups. "I'm so used to giving her what she wants, I wasn't thinking."

Beckham wiggled free and scurried under the bed.

"Sorry, we weren't expecting this." Massie shrugged with an annoying amount of nonchalance. "She's used to being the only animal."

"So is Dylan," Alicia snickered, waving away some freshly fouled air.

"So is your face," Dylan countered.

They all cracked up except Kristen. She dropped to her belly and pouted her apologies to the trembling kitty as her canine tormentor lay peacefully on a pile of pillows above.

"You may want to put Black-Tie Beckham in your mom's room." Massie plugged her flatiron into the wall and took down her ponytail. "You know, until he learns to deal." She shook out her shiny brown hair.

A flood of tears filled Kristen's eyes as she stood. "This is *his* room." Her voice trembled. "If anyone goes, it's—"

"When does Dune get back?" Claire pulled an orange gummy worm out of the bowl and slurped it like spaghetti, her blue eyes wide with innocence.

Monday! Kristen wanted to snap. Hadn't she been talking about it all week? But Claire's soft grin said she'd only asked to prevent a fight.

"Extra, extra!" Alicia jumped up on the green and white comforter and bounced, jostling Bean like a penny on a trampoline. Her C-cups Jell-Oed inside her navy babydolls. "I've got gossip!"

Kristen lowered the volume on "Wake Up Call" and plopped down beside Alicia's bare feet.

Massie, Dylan, and Claire quickly joined her.

"How many points?" Dylan poked her tongue through a chocolate-covered pretzel and waved it around.

"Five hundy." Alicia landed on her butt and crossed her toned dancer's legs.

"Granted." Massie made a note in her 3G. "Now open like a zip drive."

Kristen felt herself grinning. Finally, something big was about to go down. This sleepover had major Hall of Fame potential. The Pretty Committee would remember this night forever.

Alicia scanned the room for the spies she knew weren't there, then whispered, "Tuesday night, some girl in dirty sweats was pedaling Derrington around town on his bike." She rocked back and forth playfully, giving the news a moment to sink in.

"Ah!" Massie winced like she had a sudden gas cramp.

Dylan quickly stood and grabbed a fistful of pretzels. Claire smile-read a text from Cam. And Kristen peeked up at her ceiling, stealing a quick glance at her C.L.A.M. crush. Two more sleeps until he was back. And then *they'd* be the hot topic.

"Source?" Massie and Dylan asked at the same time.

"Apple C!" they then called immediately, both girls trying to look less affected by the news than they really were.

"Josh." Alicia beamed.

"So? Does he know who she is?" Dylan casually asked her pretzel.

"Typical." Massie sprang off the bed and returned to her flatiron.

"What?" Dylan followed her to the mirror. "What's typical?"

"Derrington ah-bviously made that up and told Josh, knowing he'd tell Leesh and Leesh would tell me." She ironed a flirty flip at the bottom of her hair. "I mean, what *real* girl would be desperate enough to pedal *him*? He's ah-bviously trying to get me jealous by self-starting a rumor."

"Ehmagawd, you're sooo right!" Dylan smacked Massie's shoulder.

"Makes sense." Claire finally looked up from her phone.

"No. It. Does. *Nawt*." Alicia smacked the comforter.

"Don't worry." Massie grinned. "You can still have your gossip points."

"Oh." Alicia smile-shrugged. "Okay."

"Maybe it's a sign." Dylan hurried for more snacks and grabbed a pita. "You know, that it's time to throw water on him and let him go."

"Not until I get Dempsey." Massie flipped off her flatiron and tousled her hair.

"But what if you don't?" Kristen blurted, and then regret-blushed.

"Don't *what*?" Massie accidentally swatted her flatiron to the floor.

"Don't get Dempsey," Claire butted in. "I mean, what if someone else likes him and, you know, gets him first?"

"Like *who*?"

"What difference does it make?" Dylan returned to the bed. "It's not like you'd go back to Derrington if you *couldn't* get Dempsey, right?"

"Given." Massie dipped her pinky in a pot of gold glitter, then wiped it on her cheekbones. "But boys are in right now. And when something's hot, I always get two."

"But what if it's true?" Dylan sat.

Massie slammed down her gold glitter, then ripped the pita from Dylan's hand. "Then that sweatpant-wearing pedal-chauffeur is done." She offered the bread to Bean, who snapped it up like a croc (the reptile, not the shoe). "Wait a minute." Her amber eyes narrowed. "I know what's going on here."

Dylan tucked a strand of already tucked hair behind her ear. Her cheeks reddened and her forehead began to leak. "What?" She stood.

"You're jealous because I'm C-plus and you're C-minus." Massie forced a pout, obviously trying to empathize. "What about that ah-dorable tennis pro you met in Hawaii?"

"Brady?" Dylan's coloring returned to normal. "Puh-lease. He's on tour for the next three years. The wait for a Prada Fairy bag isn't that long."

"When can we talk about the cheerleading squad?" Alicia placed her pumiced heel on the back of Kristen's desk chair and leaned forward to stretch. "I was thinking the moves could be mostly modern dance. It's a totally fresh take on—"

"Rate me." Massie put a hand on her hip, lifted her chin, and cocked her head. Her dark brown hair was straight and glossy. The flowing hemline of her African-print maxi-dress kissed her gold pedicure. And her cheekbones shimmered like Mount Kilimanjaro at dusk.

"Nine," Alicia blurted.

The others nodded in agreement.

Satisfied, Massie struck a pose. She rotated the left side

of her face toward the door and half smiled as if it were about to snap her photo.

"Why do you care about your rating?" Kristen asked, wondering if the alpha would admit she was hoping to see Dempsey. "It's just a sleepover."

"Why do you care about the number of goals you score?" Massie pinched her cheeks for some last minute color. "It's just a game."

"That's *different*."

"How?" Massie checked the time on her 3G. "You play to win and so do I."

"Point!" Alicia lifted her finger in the air.

"What are you trying to win?" Claire tied a red gummy worm around her ring finger.

"Hell-ooooh?" a boy's voice called from the hall outside Kristen's bedroom. "Anybody home?" He knuckle-knocked.

"*That*." Massie rolled back her shoulders and smiled like a prom queen.

Prickly heat spread throughout Kristen's entire body. Was the room hotter than seventy-six degrees? Had her antiperspirant stopped working? Were Dempsey's eyes always army green? She wiped her palms on her blue-and-white striped Victoria's Secret pajama bottoms, wishing she had worn something less . . . cotton. But her mind and body were like plaids and stripes, refusing to work together, leaving Kristen to wonder why, exactly, her internal crush furnace was overheating to such an obvious degree.

Was it:

A) The thrill of having a boy—any boy—at her first sleepover?

B) The pressure she felt to save Dempsey for Layne? Even though Massie had sprayed him?

C) Knowing on some deep subconscious level that in two days Dune would be standing in her doorway and she couldn't wait? ✓

D) Something else she didn't dare consider?

Kristen always chose C when she didn't know the answer. A sudden waft of Chanel No. 19 filled the room.

"What're you doin' here?" Kristen managed, trying to sound casual.

"He must have seen your *note*," Massie blurted sharply, alerting her to play along. "You know, the one you *slid* under his *door* that said to *stop by* and *let us know* if you made the *team*. Heart—*only as a friend*—Kristen?"

"Oh yeah." Kristen blushed again. "So, *did* you make it?"

Dempsey stepped into the room. His dirty blond hair was sweaty and matted. His black soccer shorts were perfectly baggy, his cheeks ah-dorably pink. Why did he have to look so soccerlicious?

"Yup." He grinned. "I quit the play and everything. There'll be another one next semester."

"Yayyyyyyy!" The girls applauded.

He smiled wide, like someone who had no clue he'd just broken Layne's heart.

"Congratulations, cheerleaders, that was your first official cheer," Massie said in her coachiest voice.

"Is this the *whole* squad?" Dempsey chuckled, helping himself to a handful of "Italian popcorn" as he scanned the other snack options.

"Tryouts are on Monday," Massie spoke up before anyone else could.

"But we're automatically in, right?" Alicia leaned, restretching her stretched hamstring.

"Given." Massie gave her a reassuring shoulder tap. "But we still have to hold auditions."

"To give everyone a fair chance?" Claire tightened her ponytail.

"No, Kuh-laire. To find LBRs for the bottom of the pyramid."

"Opposite of a good idea." Alicia stood up on Kristen's bed.

"'Scuse me?" Massie lifted an eyebrow.

"Pyramids are out. But don't worry. I'll show you some sequences I learned at Body Alive and—"

Massie side-glanced at Dempsey, then stood. "Um, Alicia, are you on the track team?"

Alicia took a step back. "No."

Massie stepped forward. "Then why are you trying to run with this?"

Everyone burst out laughing.

"I'm gonna tell Layne to audition." Dempsey examined the bowl of Sweet 'n' Salty Surprise with delight. "She was just telling me what a huge soccer fan she is."

"Sad times ten." Massie fake-sulked. "But our practices will conflict with play rehearsals, so—"

"It's okay!" Dempsey grabbed Kristen's soccer ball off her trophy shelf and spun it until the black and white patches blurred. "We made a pact. We both dropped out of the play so we could be in the next one together. I bet she'd love to be on your squad."

Kristen's stomach lurched. *OMG! He likes Layne!*

"But she doesn't have any dance training," Alicia whined.

"Massie can teach anyone anything." Dempsey smiled fondly at the alpha.

Kristen's stomach lurched again. *OMG! He likes Massie!*

She peeked at Claire, who was scrutinizing the cuticle on her left thumb. Did she feel uncomfortable too? Burdened with too much information and doomed to carry the weight of that knowledge alone?

Claire *had* to know how Layne felt about Dempsey. After all, they were best friends OTPC (Outside The Pretty Committee). And *everyone* knew how Massie felt.

If only she could ask Claire's advice. She'd want to know:

A) Which friend did she feel more obligated to help?
B) What was the best way to ask Dempsey who he liked?
C) Who did she think liked him more, Massie or Layne?
D) Who did she think deserved him more, Massie or Layne?
E) Who did she think was a better match for him, Massie or Layne?
F) Could she trust her enough to tell her about the Witty Committee?
G) All of the above. ✓

Yes, Claire had kept Kristen's scholarship secret, but conspiracy to cover a friendship with an LBR? That was a serious *Mass*demeanor.

"This is gonna be so cool!" Dempsey clapped once.

Yeah! If you considered . . .

A) Being a double agent for your friends while they crush on the same guy COOL!

C) Pretending soccer has cheerleaders so your BFF can stalk a player COOL!

C) All of the above COOL! ✓

Then sure, this was gonna be great!

Massie mounted her bamboo eco-chair and clapped twice. "Qui-eeeeet!"

Fifty-eight cheerleader-wannabes stopped gossiping at once.

"Good." Massie grinned, pleased that the glitter-dusted hopefuls honored Rule No. 1 of her audition contract—*Obey What I Say*.

The rest of the Pretty Committee sat on either side of her, *American Idol* style, pens and stacks of purple paper laid neatly in front of them. They were wearing their cheerleader uniforms, which, thanks to Massie's purple hair streak, had been designed and delivered by Stella McCartney in less than forty-eight hours. And, thanks to Massie's explicit directions, they looked nuh-thing like cheerleader uniforms.

Black sequined off-the-shoulder minidresses with THE SOCC-HERS spelled in gold-stitched letters were sure to be envied, even from the cheap seats. Underneath, the Pretty Committee wore black leather short shorts, because no one wanted to stumble on a mid-flip crotch shot of herself on the Internet. And, in keeping with the Tomahawks' American Indian theme, they wore knee-high metallic gold moccasins with festive bells dangling off the fringes. Butt-sweeping ponytail extensions took care of their hair—bronzing gel and MAC took care of the rest.

The Massie-quin stood proudly at the end of the judges' table, dressed in one of the three remaining uniforms.

"As I mentioned in my weekend e-mail blast," Massie began, already feeling very captain-ish, "you will approach the table, recite your two-line cheer, and tell us in one word what you think you'd add to my squad."

An anxious murmur was building among the dense crowd. Massie suddenly realized it would take hours to get through everyone. By then, Pinkberry would be closed, Bean would have peed her doggy Diesels, and Dempsey would be logged off for the night.

She lifted a finger, informing the wannabes to wait one more minute.

"Change of plan," she whispered to the PC. "Each one of you gets to handpick one person to audition. The rest will have to go."

The girls opened their mouths in protest. Massie silenced them with a palm.

"Look for stocky ones who look like they could hold a lot of weight on their shoulders. The more they look like Chicken McNuggets, the better. "

"McNuggetttttts," Dylan burped.

Massie elbowed her in the McRib. "Lady behavior!" she hissed.

"I already told you." Alicia tugged her long ponytail in frustration. "Pyramids are out!"

Massie lifted her palm again. "TCHS."

"*What?*" Alicia snapped.

"The Captain Has Spoken."

Alicia rolled her eyes and sighed while Massie made a mental note to eliminate pyramids from her routine. Then she made a second mental note: Convince everyone it had been her idea.

They spent the next ten minutes walking the line and making their selections. Five lucky girls and one thin boy were invited to the table. The remaining fifty-two stormed off in an angry huff—leaving behind a sandstorm of multicolored glitter and a howling gale of lawsuit threats.

"First in line, please approach the judges." Massie restacked her stacked paper as a short-legged baby-faced girl with light brown eyes and a sea blue Juicy sweat suit marched forward. "Who selected you?" Massie tapped the cap of her purple metallic pen against her teeth.

"I did." Kristen lifted her hand from the far left side of the table. "This is Ripple. She's very athletic and totally available after school and—"

"Like *six* years old!" Massie snapped.

"Point!" Alicia lifted her finger.

"Nine!" Ripple corrected.

"Do you even *go* here?" Dylan twirled her ultra-thick, half-straight, half-curly ponytail.

"Not yet, but I will." She beamed. "And when I do, I'm going to start my own Pretty Committee and cheerleading squad and surf team and—"

"Um, Ripple, are you asleep?"

Ripple peered at Kristen, hoping for clarification. Kristen lowered her eyes, offering none.

"No." She giggled nervously. "Why?"

"Then why are you dreaming?" Massie glared at Kristen, reprimanding her for making such a ridiculous choice. With a name like that, she *had* to be related to Dune.

"Don't you want to hear my cheer?"

Everyone shook their heads no.

"What about my one word?"

They shook their heads again.

"It's *youth*," Ripple tried. "I will bring youth to the team." She stuck out her flat chest with pride.

Massie stood and put her hands on her sequin-covered hips. "Opposite of please stay or I will make sure everyone knows to love you when you go here."

"Huh?" Ripple tugged the zipper on her sweatshirt.

"Leave!" Massie hissed.

"But she's wearing my brother's necklace," Ripple whined. "You *have* to pick me."

"I *knew* it!" Massie stabbed the table with her purple pen.

"You better go," Kristen mumbled.

"I'm telling my brother!" She stomped out in last summer's J. Crew flip-flops.

Massie was about to scold Kristen for putting the team at risk to further her crush-life, but thought better of it when she saw the next person on line.

"Step forward," she mumbled.

Layne and the tall, thin, redheaded boy Massie had nick-named Twizzler approached the table. They wore matching white unitards covered in black hexagons, looking like two soccer balls that had been flattened by a steamroller.

"Our word is *flair*," Layne stated.

"Nice pick, Kuh-laire," Alicia muttered.

"I didn't pick them," Claire whispered back.

"Did you?" Alicia whisper-asked Dylan.

"Puh-lease!" Dylan rolled her eyes.

"You?" she asked Kristen.

"I did," Massie barked. "Now let her finish."

"Thank you." Layne nodded. "And now for our cheer."

Layne unrolled two blue gym mats while Twizzler rubbed chalk on his hands. Once the mats were down, he lay on his back and lifted his limbs like a dog playing dead. Standing above him, Layne clasped his feet with her hands while he clasped hers with his. In a show of tremendous physical strength, they fused together into a giant letter O and began rolling down the mat chanting: "Juggle, dribble, kick. The Tomahawks are slick! Juggle, dribble, kick. The Tomahawks are slick! Juggle, dribble, kick. The Tomahawks are slick. . . ."

The other wannabes jumped out of their way.

"I once saw six midgets do that in Cirque du Soleil," Alicia gasped.

"Cirque du No Way!" Dylan giggled as they rolled past her.

"Are they supposed to be a soccer ball?" Claire's blue eyes were wide with amazement.

"More like a *psycho* ball." Alicia cracked up.

Kristen jumped to her feet. "Look out for the—"

They smashed into the juice kiosk with an audible yelp.

"Opposite of an option, right?" Alicia knit her dark brows.

"Congratulations, Layne and Twizzler," Massie announced as two Chicken McNuggets helped them to their feet. "You're official Socc-Hers."

"What?" Alicia snapped.

"We need *flair*," Massie insisted, hoping she sounded sincere. "And everyone loves a guy in a dress. All in favor?"

Massie, Claire, and Kristen raised their hands.

"Majority wins."

Layne and Twizzler jump-hugged.

"Check your in-boxes for a rehearsal schedule," Massie stated, then waved them off. "Next."

"Wait, are you serious?" Alicia asked, clearly unable to let it go.

Massie avoided her pleading dark eyes. But the inability to lie was her only flaw. "I am."

"How? Why?"

"Because." She rolled her eyes. "Layne ah-bviously *likes* Dempsey. But if I keep her busy in Socc-Hers rehearsals, she won't have time to hang out with him."

"Fine, but do we need the guy?" Alicia muttered under her cinnamon-scented breath.

Massie inhaled slowly to avoid losing her patience in front of the squad. "Yes, we need the *guy*. If Layne rolls around with Twizz every day after school, maybe she'll forget all about Dempsey and—"

Alicia grabbed Massie's sequin-covered shoulders and looked her straight in the eye. "You don't hawnestly think *Layme* is competition. *Do you?*"

Massie stepped out from under her grip. "Dempsey used to be an LBR, remember?" she whispered.

Alicia nodded yes.

"Welllllll." Massie paused to make sure no one was eaves-dropping. "Even though he's been cured, he may still have trace amounts of LBR in his blood. And hanging around Layne could activate those trace amounts. And once they're reacti-vated, he'll assume I'm out of his league and he'll settle for her. Which rules *me* out."

Alicia nodded her head while considering this, then lifted her finger. "Point."

"Thank you." Massie sighed. "Now can we *puh-lease* move on?"

Without waiting for an answer she shouted, *"Next!"*

Olivia Ryan stepped forward. Her pleated white miniskirt, turquoise bikini top, and gray Capezio dance heels reminded Massie why she couldn't stand the girl. Physically, she was a natural fit for the Pretty Committee. Her blond wavy hair, navy blue eyes, and perfect dancer's body made the choice a no-brainer. Unfortunately, Olivia was a no-brainer with no style, and the PC had a strict "no airhead" policy. She was a B-lister trapped in an A-lister's body.

"Hi, I'm Olivia Ryan and my one word is *people skills and dance training*."

Kristen burst out laughing. "Her word should be *stoopid*."

"I object!" Claire slammed her fist on the table. "I don't want her on the team."

"Why?" Alicia stood.

"She stole Cam," Claire whisper-hissed.

"You broke *up*," Alicia countered. "Besides, she's the second-best dancer in our grade. We need her."

"Well, I can't work with her," Claire huffed.

"Then she's gone," Massie stated.

Alicia's mouth opened like she was about to projectile.

"We made a pledge, Leesh." Massie gripped the purple letters on her key chain. "PC support means we take care of each other first."

"But—"

"Butts are for kicking. Now, do you want to kick her out or should I?"

Alicia shrugged petulantly.

"Fine." Massie invited Olivia to step closer with the slow curl of her finger. She glared into the girl's vacant navy eyes and grinned with devilish anticipation. "Do you have violent tendencies?"

Olivia shook her head no.

"Then why were you hitting on Cam Fisher?"

Claire giggled.

"What does this have to do with *Cam*?"

"Nuh-thing." Massie rolled her eyes in frustration. "It has to do with *Kuh-laire*. Now leave before I have you arrested for attempted robbery."

"That's not fair!"

"If you want *fair*, look at your pasty face in the mirror. If you want to keep the 'live' in Olivia, leave now!"

The girl turned on the heel of her Capezio and clacked out of the café, the pleats on her skirt waving goodbye with every angry step she took. "You're not a cheerleader, you're a *fear*-leader!" she called, then slammed the door behind her.

"You're an *I.Q.-of-a-deer*-leader," Massie called.

Kristen burst out laughing.

"*Queer*-leader!" Dylan burped.

"Ew, *not-in-my-ear-leader*!" Kristen cackled.

Everyone laughed except Alicia.

"Thank you." Claire smiled appreciatively.

"Yeah, thanks," Alicia grumbled.

"Leesh, are you an LBR with a broken leg?"

"No."

"Then stop acting like a sore loser and let's move on," Massie insisted. She was about to summon the next wannabe when her left cheek started to burn.

She turned toward the heat. It was coming from Claire's eyeballs. Or rather, from the "I adore Massie" love rays beaming out of them.

"What are you *doing*?"

"I can't believe you stood up for me like that?" Claire effused.

Massie rolled her eyes. "That's what friends do, *Kuh-laire*. They look out for each other. Right, girls?"

"Right," they mumbled, almost like they didn't mean it.

"Now stop *staring*!" Massie barked. And then her iPod chimed. "Ehma-*text*! It's from Dempsey."

Dempsey: Got squad?

Massie began typing, blurring the touch screen with her sweaty fingerprints.

Gawd, what was it about the ex-LBR that made her intestines undulate? Her palms dribble? Her heart stutter? Her lips hunger for gloss? And her brain think Layne Abeley was actually a threat?

Massie: Gimme a Y!
Dempsey: Y
Massie: E!
Dempsey: E
Massie: Ssssss!
Dempsey: Ssssss!
Massie: Whaddaya Got?
Dempsey: ☺

Massie's entire body smiled back. Gawd, what was it about him that made her lose her cool like Tom Cruise on *Oprah*? His ah-dorable dimples? His army green eyes? His knack for makeovers? His family embracing the African orphan trend? His leading role in the school play? His raw soccer talent? His ability to shed twenty pounds in a single summer? *WHAAAAT?????*

Unlike Derrington, who was good from afar but far from good, Dempsey was good no matter how close you were standing. He was an alpha male who'd shed his LBR skin and then buried it out back where no one could find it.

Ehma-crush! Thoughts of Dempsey made Massie's leg shake anxiously. It was time to wrap this up and get back to their textual relationship.

"You, over there." She pointed at one of the remaining two girls, recognizing her stocky little body from gymnastics. Her hair was dirty blond, her T-zone was clear, and her teeth were even. She was a solid seven out of ten; pretty enough to be seen with but not a threat. "Congratulations, McNugget Number One, you're a Socc-Her."

"Yayyy," Claire squeaked, air-clapping for her pick.

McNugget No. 1 stepped forward. "My name is—"

"What about *me*?" McNugget No. 2 whined. "I didn't even get to try out."

"Next season." Massie tried to smile sweetly. It looked like the sun was in her eyes.

"Why her?" Alicia cocked her head and blinked rapidly.

"Why nawt?" Massie cocked back.

"It's like you *want* your teammates to look bad," Alicia snipped.

"I do." Massie began gathering the stacks of unused paper.

"Why?"

"So we look *good*." She playfully smacked Alicia's butt-length ponytail.

But instead of raising her finger and saying "Point," Alicia steadied her swinging hair and walked out.

Kristen triple-pushed the elevator button. If she could just get upstairs and change out of her Socc-Hers uniform before her mother got home, she'd never, ever, *ev-er*, be too lazy to Range-change again. This time she meant it. *Pinky-swear!*

She hyper-pushed the up arrow for the eighty-third time.

"Miss Gregory?" Willard, the building's door attendant, asked politely.

OMG, Mom! Marsha must have been walking in behind her! Maydayyyyyy!

Kristen speed-ducked behind the waxy green leaves of the lobby ficus.

"Miss Gregory!" Willard called. "Who ya hiding from? The fashion police?" He chuckled, the stubbly pink skin below his chin reverberating with glee. If Kristen hadn't been so embarrassed, she might have laughed too.

"Oh, no one." She emerged, cheeks on fire. "Forget it."

"If it's a handsome boy about your age, you're too late. He already went up to your floor." He winked.

Kristen's insides did the wave. "*What* boy?"

"The boy who dropped this." Willard shuffled over to Kristen and handed her a worn leather cuff with the letter *D* scratched into the center. Was it Dempsey's?

Finally, the elevator stuttered open.

"I'll take it to him." Kristen grabbed the cuff and hurried inside. "Thanks," she called, pushing door-close with finger-whitening intensity.

The inside of the elevator smelled faintly of coconuts. Instinctively, Kristen reached for her necklace and ran the shark tooth back and forth across the leather strap. According to the crumpled itinerary at the bottom of her soccer bag, Dune should have landed two hours ago.

Kristen checked her messages . . . again. Still no "I'm home" text.

But instead of questioning Dune's feelings for her—something she normally would have done—her thoughts returned instantly to the *D* cuff sealed inside her sweaty fist.

What was it about her new neighbor that made her skin buzz? It had to be the anxiety she felt knowing both Layne and Massie were counting on her to play cupid. It *had* to be.

After a slight jerk, the doors parted. Kristen headed straight for 10G, overcome by the sudden urge to run. She knocked gently even though she wanted to pound.

Dempsey opened the door immediately. Amber-scented incense filled the hall. "Hey." He smiled, his eyes even greener than they'd been at lunch. "Cool uniform."

Kristen pinched her sequin-covered dress. "Oh yeah." She blushed.

"Did Massie design them?" His face illuminated when he said her name.

Kristen nodded yes.

"Wow," he mouthed, scanning her.

Was he impressed because he thought:

A) Massie was talented?

B) Massie was insane?

C) He thought Kristen looked hawt?

D) He thought Kristen looked like Las Vegas?

E) No idea whatsoever. ✓

"What?" Kristen asked self-consciously.

"This whole cheerleading thing is awesome." He gave her a hearty thumbs-up.

"Really?" She grinned. "You don't think it's lame?"

"What's lame about having the coolest girls at school cheering while you're playing soccer?" He glanced at his bare feet, then lifted his head with a hopeful grin. "Hey, we should all go to Rye Playland this weekend. You know, the soccer team and the cheerleaders. My parents rented out the park so they could take some visiting orphans. It should be pretty cool."

Kristen slowly began to relax, like an overblown balloon with a tiny leak. "Sure." She considered asking him which cheerleader he thought was the "coolest." Which one he wanted to sit beside on the Dragon Coaster. Which one he was really asking out. But Kristen stopped herself when she heard his mom.

"Dempsey!" she shouted. "Come set the table."

This time *he* blushed. "I better go."

"Oh, I almost forgot." Kristen held out her hand. "You dropped your bracelet in the lobby."

Dempsey eyed the sweaty cuff. "'That's not mine. I don't do real leather."

"It's nawt?" *OMG!* If it wasn't Dempsey's, that meant the *D* stood for . . .

"Dempseeeeeey."

"Better go." He rolled his eyes. "See ya tomorrow?"

Kristen nodded yes as he shut the door.

"It's mine," declared a familiar boy's voice.

Kristen whip-turned, her heart beating double-time. *"EhMaGawd!"*

Dune was sitting Indian-style on the floor reading a *Silver Surfer* comic book. His skin was so tanned she could barely see him in the dimly lit hallway.

"Nice necklace." He smiled shyly.

"You're here!" Kristen stood above him awkwardly while her internal hard drive rebooted.

His bracelet.

Her crush.

Dune Baxter.

Back from Tavarua.

She had waited weeks for this moment.

Imagined it playing out a billion different ways.

Yet not one of them like this.

Kristen had no idea if she should:

A) Ask how his trip was?
B) Wait for him to stand?
C) Lean down?

D) Hug him?

E) Kiss him?

F) If E, then lip or cheek?

G) Start talking about the first thing that came to her mind to avoid making a decision she'd probably regret? ✓

"Dude, you have no idea what's been going on," she prattled with hushed urgency, in case Dempsey could hear.

"What?" He stood, like his help might be called upon any minute.

"LayneandMassiebothlikemyneighborDempseyandtheybothwantmetotalktohimforthem.IshouldhelpMassiebecause she'smyBFFbutMassiedoesn'tknowI'mfriendswithLayne andLaynesaidIoweherbigtimewhichIdobecauseshehelpedmeget—" Kristen stopped before she revealed too much. "Anyway"—she sighed—"I don't know what to do."

"Easy." Dune stuffed the comic book in the back pocket of his baggy faded Hurley jeans. "Massie probably likes him because he's trendy. She'll find someone else. Help Layne. She's cooler."

Kristen smiled. Even though his advice was helpful minus fifty, it was good to have her voice of reason back. Dune had a good (-looking!) head on his shoulders.

"So." He flicked her ponytail. "Your hair grew a *lot*."

"It's fake." Kristen giggled, then immediately wished she'd chosen a different word. "It's my cheerleading costume."

"Cheerleading?"

"Yeah, I know." Kristen rolled her eyes. "It's this new thing we're kind of doing as an experiment."

"You look like an OCDiva," he told her long bare legs.

"That's not all she looks like."

"Mom?" Kristen gasp-turned.

Marsha was standing behind them gripping a brown bag of groceries, nibbling her lower lip. "Hi, Dune, welcome home. It's lovely to see you. Now leave."

"But *Mom!*"

Marsha cupped her ear. "I'm sorry, did you hear an *ex-*cheerleader say something?"

"Mom, I can explain."

"Goodbye, Dune."

He backed into the elevator as if Marsha's forceful glare were pushing him.

As the doors closed, Dune wiggled his thumbs, letting Kristen know he'd text her later.

"Your bracelet!" She waved the cuff, but it was too late. Dune was gone.

"Inside!" Marsha insisted, turning her key while balancing the grocery bag on her knee.

"But—" Kristen began, and then stopped. She probably could have convinced her mother to let her run after Dune and return his leather *D*. But for some reason, she just didn't feel like it.

Dylan examined Massie's rehearsal schedule. But only to anchor her eyeballs and keep them from drifting toward the boy seated behind her. Not that it was helping. His dirty blond ah-dorableness lured her pupils like ships to the Bermuda triangle . . . extensions to Jessica Simpson . . . adoptions to Hollywood.

SOCC-HERS REHEARSAL SCHEDULE
Week of 9/28–10/2

MONDAY

Time: 4:00 p.m.–5:00 p.m.
Place: The New Green Café

- Auditions.

Time: 8:00 p.m.
Place: Your own house

- Check in-boxes for this schedule.

- Massie reviews popular dance movies such as *Dirty Dancing, Save the Last Dance, Bring It On, Stomp the Yard, Step Up, Step Up 2: The Streets, Bossa Nova, Planet B-Boy*.

- Massie finalizes routines and cheers. Note: I have decided that pyramids are no longer part of the program. I'm over them. If you had your heart set on them, please let me know ASAP so I can replace you.

TUESDAY

Time: 4:00 p.m.–7:30 p.m.
Place: The Block Estate

- Massie teaches cheers.

Time: 9:00 p.m.–11:00 p.m.
Place: Your own house

- Practice on your own. Note: Draw blinds so wannabes can't copy.

- Stretch for 30 minutes, then take a bath with Epsom salts.

- Pat dry.

- Moisturize.

WEDNESDAY

Time: 7:00 a.m.–8:10 a.m.
Place: BOCD

- Mellow rehearsal on the field. Avoid sweating because we won't have time to shower until after third-period Pilates.

Time: 4:00 p.m.–7:30 p.m.
Place: The Block Estate

- Walk the grounds practicing step-clapping and speaking in clear, distinct syllables.

- ** Example: (clap) This (clap-clap) sounds (clap-clap clap-clap) ea- (clap) si- (clap) er (clap-clap) than it is (clap-clap clap-clap CLAP!)

THURSDAY

Time: 7:00 am–8:10 am
Place: BOCD pool

- Aqua rehearsal to loosen muscles and test acoustics in echo-y pool.

Time: 4:00 p.m.–5:00 p.m.
Place: Longshadows Nursing Home

- Dress rehearsal for super-old people.
** Remember to smile and e-nun-ci-ate.

Time: 5:15 p.m.–5:30 p.m.
Place: The Block Estate

- Massie meets publicist Antonia Coburn at the Block estate to get Captain photo taken for local papers.

Time: 5:30 p.m.–7:30 p.m.

- Review feedback from Longshadows. Fine-tune.

FRIDAY

Time: 6:30 am–8:00 am
Place: The Block Estate

- Uniform fittings by Inez, the Blocks'
  housekeeper, as some outfits may need to be
  taken in due to an increase in burned calories.
  (Fingers crossed!)

** If an outfit needs to be let out, you will be
  off the team. I can easily replace you. Hair and
  makeup by Jakkob. Try not to move or eat for
  the rest of the day.

Time: 4:15 p.m.
Place: Sirens-Tomahawks field

- Massie gives out special pom-poms. Manicures,
  please.

Time: 4:30 p.m.

- Kickoff! Tomahawks vs. Groundhogs.
  Goooooo Socc-Hers!

Time: 5:30 p.m.

- Greet the fans. Smile and pack Purell. They can
  be dirty.

It had been a hectic week, filled with Socc-Her boot camp and staccato clapping. But nawt a single glorious detention. Sadly, Dylan's flirt time with Derrick had dropped to a record low. And so had Dylan. Communication had been limited to passing hallway smiles, which ultimately needed to be dissected and analyzed, robbing Dylan of her much-needed beauty sleep.

Their text life had suffered too. He'd sent one message that said: "Sister loved the b-day presents. Thx." To which Dylan had replied "Yay!" and then hated herself for not writing something more conversational like, "What did she say?" or "Which gift was her fave?" or "Wanna lip-kiss?" Every time she passed the parking lot pigeons—*their* parking lot pigeons—a little piece of her died.

More than anything, Dylan wanted to ask Massie for advice. *Should she text him? Search for a "lost contact lens" by his trailer when class let out? Was he just not that into her?* But more than anything, she knew she couldn't. The whole predicament weighed heavier than the mandatory hair extension clipped to her naturally thick ponytail.

The stands were filling up with families, teachers, and students, each clamoring to get a good view of the field and a better view of the cheerleaders.

Clap-clap!

"Huddle!" Massie called extra loud, obviously playing to the ogling fans.

The Socc-Hers padded toward her, sounding more like Santa's helpers than spirit providers, thanks to the fringe-bells on their gold moccasins.

Lucky Kristen! Dylan thought as her mom-benched friend lifted Derrick's propped leg like a drawbridge and took the seat beside him.

"Team," Massie began sternly, "you have worked long and hard this week. And to show you how proud I am, I replaced your regular pom-poms with . . . " She dumped her Juicy "Nice Girls" tote in the center of their huddle. A stack of fourteen iridescent plume–covered bags landed in a luxurious heap. "Peacock feather–covered clutches!"

"You each get two," Massie announced with pride. "And when cheerleading season is over you can totally use them for black-tie occasions."

Everyone squealed with joy, except Twizzler, who blushed. And Layne, who sneezed.

"I have given you the best outfits. The best hair and makeup. The best pom-poms. The best cheers. The best choreography and—"

Echu-echu. Alicia fake-coughed.

Massie responded with an amber-colored death glare.

"—Aaaand," she continued, "the best of myself. The rest is up to you. So let's *(clap)* give *(clap)* these *(clap-clap)* Socc-*(clap)*Her *(clap)* fans *(clap-clap)* something *(clap-clap-clap-clap-clap)* to cheeeeeer about! *WE'RE. SOCC-HER! WE'RE, WE'RE. SOCC-HER. . . ."* She began cheering, and the squad joined in with explosive team spirit, punching the crisp fall air with their peacock-feather bags and circulating it with swings of their ponytails.

"WE'RE. SOCC-HER!
WE'RE, WE'RE. SOCC-HER!
IF YOU'RE COLD SAY BURRRR.
IF YOU'RE A CAT SAY PURRR.
PARDONNEZ-MOI, MONSIEUR—
JE M'APPELLE *SOCC-HER!*
YAYYYY!"

The crowd cheered. Massie bowed. Derrington hopped up on one leg and wiggled his butt. Dylan melted.

The players began taking the field. Claire and Alicia cheered wildly when Cam and Josh ran out.

"It's go time, team." Massie took a hearty swig of Evian and swallowed with an Olympic-size "Ahhhhhhh." Rejuvenated, she smacked the cap back on the bottle and got serious. "McNugget, move your hips. Twizzler, less arm-swing. Layne, get a tissue. Kuh-laire, more pop. Dylan, sharper head snaps. Alicia, stop counting us in. That's my job." She took another sip. Waves of imported springwater glistened inside the blue-tinted bottle as it slanted toward her glossy lips.

Gawd! What a waste of power, Dylan thought. *She's drinking my future. Swallowing my crush!*

If only Massie would have the decency to dump the refreshing taste of the French Alps on Derrington. Splash him with liberty and douse him with desire. He'd be free! . . . Free to limp-run onto the field . . . free to profess his Dylan-love . . . free to lip-kiss her in front of—

The crunch of an empty water bottle slapped her back to reality.

"Missing something?" Massie held a thick red horsetail under Dylan's chin.

"Oops." Dylan took the two-pound extension. "It must have fallen off," she sighed, reluctantly clipping it back into place.

"You know, Dylan"—Alicia stretched her hammy, launching the jingle of a hundred little bells—"you should really be more careful. And Massie, as captain, you should be more strict."

"Seriously?" Dylan laughed the word out of her mouth, covering it in utter disbelief. It was one thing to be treated like a child by her best friend. But it was *two* things to be standing near a new crush while she was doing it.

"Yeah, *seriously*." Alicia stretched her other leg. "We're seconds away from curtain. Massie, you need to feel confident that your dancers are ready to take the stage. I advise you not to rescue them anymore. If they mess up, they pack up."

Massie put her hands on her hips and thrust her neck like a chicken mid-peck. "And I advise *you* nawt to advise *me.* Ever. *Ah*-gain!"

"Funny *you* should talk about rescuing, Leesh," Dylan blurted.

"Whaddaya mean?" Alicia's heavily lined eyes narrowed. She rested her arm on the metal frame of the Tomahawks' goalie net, or whatever that thing was called.

"I *mean*"—she cranked up the volume—"weren't you

telling everyone in French that you *rescued* Massie? And that without your *input* these *routines* would be sixth-grade level?"

"Opposite of true!" Alicia stomped her moccasin, a jingle punctuating her rage. "You know I don't speak French."

Despite the weight of her ponytail, Dylan cocked her head. "French *class*." She paused. "You know the one with Josh and Cam and Derrington, and—"

"—and taking the place of our injured captain," bellowed the student sportscaster, "our newest player, Dempsey Solomon!"

"Moving awn!" Massie shouted at her friends, then lifted her peacock feather–covered clutches. "We've got a job to do, girls."

"Hey!"

"And Twizzler." She drew back her lips and forced a big, toothy smile, looking more like a dentist's mold than a cheer-leader. "Ready? And!"

The Socc-Hers scurried into position.

"Ah five, ah six, ah five, six, sev-uhn, eight!"

"DEMPSEY LEARNED SOCCER IN AFRICA,
HE'S KING OF THE FIELD, RAAAA RAAA RAAA!
DEMPSEY LEARNED SOCCER IN AFRICA,
HE'S KING OF THE FIELD, RAAAA RAAA RAAA!
DEMPSEY LEARNED SOCC—"

Layne waved her clutches with such excitement they hit Massie on the cheek.

*"—ER IN AFRICA,
HE'S KING OF THE FIELD, RAAAA RAAA RAAA."*

Massie responded by hip-bumping Layne into Twizzler, then jamming her clutches in Layne's nostrils. Layne triple-sneezed in her face.

*"DEMPSEY LEARNED SOCCER IN AFRICA,
HE'S KING OF THE FIELD, RAAAA RAAA RAAA!"*

"Ew! Stop!" Massie squealed, unintentionally ending the cheer.

"I think I'm allergic." Layne sniffled.

"Really?" The corners of Massie's lips curled in serendipitous delight. "How lucky."

MSG had taken the field, and suddenly twenty-two hawt boys were chasing a ball.

"Go, Dempsey!" Layne shrieked, wiping her nose.

"Formation steamroller!" Massie called, mashing her feathers in Layne's face like it was on fire.

"Aaahhh-chhhooo!" Layne sneezed with the force of a Mega Power 4000 hair dryer. Her ponytail cast forward like a fishing reel and wrapped around the goalie's net. "Ow, my head!"

Twizzler, McNugget, and Claire worked quickly to release her. Once Layne was free, Nurse Adele held an ice pack to her scalp and guided her off the field.

Twizzler followed dutifully, carrying Layne's clutches.

"Stay with the team," Layne strained like someone who'd been lost in the desert.

"But—"

"They *need* you," she choked.

Twizzler looked at the squad, then back at Layne, clearly questioning his priorities, evaluating his usefulness, and consulting his moral compass. Then, with a soldier's sense of duty, he blew Layne a two-fingered kiss and jogged off to complete his mission.

"Steeeeeam*roller*!" Massie called with renewed energy.

Twizzler dropped down on all fours and looked up at Massie. "We need someone to be Layne."

"What about Dylan?" Alicia offered.

"Why *me*?" she asked, pulling a tube of clear Lancôme gloss from her feather clutch pom-pom.

"Your back is pretty, you know . . . *wide*."

Dylan's fingers began to throb. Was this how the Incredible Hulk felt before his shirt ripped open?

"And if we're gonna steamroll over someone I think it should be—"

"Why don't you lie on your back in case someone falls?" Dylan blurted. "We can use your boobs as cushions."

Dempsey ran by kicking the ball.

"New cheer!" Massie called with fake enthusiasm. "Designer Girls! And . . . "

They lifted their clutches, matched her fake smile, and began.

"ADIDAS, FILA, NIKE TOO:

WHAT'S A SOCC-HER GIRL TO DO?
WE GOTTA LOOK HAWT FOR THE FELLAS—
THAT'S WHY WE'RE ALL WEARING STELLAS!"

Sensing Derrick was watching, Dylan swung her head like a Garnier Fructis model, reminding him that, with or without the heavy extension, she still had the thickest hair in the eighth grade.

The louder he cheered, the harder she swung. Until, suddenly, her head felt lighter. Like she had been transported into a real commercial where hair moved like it was submerged in water and felt luxuriously weightless.

"Ahhhhh," Alicia shouted, tripping on a chunk of red hair. She caught herself before falling but still, everyone in the first row was laughing.

"Hey!" Dylan shout-pointed at the ground. "That's mine!"

"You're *dead*," Alicia hissed, rotating her almost-sprained ankle.

Tired of fighting, Dylan burped "Deeeeadddddd" right in Alicia's face.

Not that it helped. Alicia gasped in disgust, then turned sharply, whipping Dylan's jaw with the bottom of her ponytail.

Despite the sudden sting, Dylan laughed. But only because Derrick was waving.

Dylan smile-waved back, noticing only after fifteen solid seconds of nonstop waving that Derrick was looking slightly past her. Like a blind man on a date.

Amid the explosive cheers of a very excited crowd—had someone scored?—Dylan tracked Derrick's warped gaze to a slightly older blonde with a pixie haircut, a flirty off-the-shoulder mint green top, two striped scarves tied around her graceful neck, and gray matchstick jeans so skinny they could have picked spinach from a tooth. She had looks, style, and enough confidence for short hair—the girl was a perfect storm.

Pulling the leather short shorts out of her butt crack, Dylan spent what seemed like the next half hour wondering how much better her life would be if she had the face for pixie cuts and the legs for stovepipes. After a blur of soulless cheering and extreme self-loathing, the game was finally over.

Judging by the high-fiving Tomahawks, Briarwood won. Reporters from BOCD's school paper, website, blog, and weekly sports newsletter surrounded the players, while the cameramen lined up to photograph the cheerleaders.

"You guys were ah-mazing!" Kristen appeared, throwing her arms around Massie with genuine sincerity.

Bending her knees, Massie lined up their eyebrows just like they do in the *New York Times* wedding section, then smiled for the camera. "Say heyyyyyy!"

"Heyyyyy!"

The flashes flashed. "Two captains!" Massie noted, in case the school paper needed help captioning the photo. Then she unhooked Kristen with a gentle nudge.

"Good job today, team." She air-clapped. "Now go check on Layne. *Stat!*"

Without hesitation Twizzler, McNugget, and Claire bolted for Nurse Adele's office, leaving Massie to model her uniform, pom-pom clutch, moccasins, and ponytail extension for the weekend style section.

Alicia inched toward the flashing cameras, her smile slick with gloss. But like an old lady shuffling toward the only available stall in a crowded bathroom, Massie "accidentally" knocked her out of the way.

Derrington and the Perfect Storm were still talking in the bleachers. She helped him stand and he put his arms around her for balance. Normally Dylan would have asked around to find out her story. But her love was forbidden, forcing her to work alone. Dylan looked around quickly to make sure no one was watching her.

"Derrick!" she called, her tone basking in sunshine.

He lifted his palm.

Propelled by her speeding pulse, she kangarooed up to the bleachers. "Hey!" she beamed, as if completely unthreatened, even though she completely *was*.

Perfect Storm knit her perfect brows and side-glanced at Derrick in a "who's the Red Bull addict?" sort of way. Dylan took *some* comfort in knowing Massie would eventually destroy Perfect Storm, but not much.

"So," Dylan stalled, searching for the perfect opener. "I've, um, been meaning to ask you. . . . Did uh . . . your sister like the birthday presents?" she said, even though he had already texted the answer earlier in the week. "You know, the ones we bought *together*?"

He looked at Perfect Storm, who giggled.

Dylan felt like she swallowed her feathery pom-pom clutch. She knew it! She was way too *ew* to get an alpha male. Her bones were t-*ew* big. Her hair was t-*ew* thick. Her skin was t-*ew* pale. Her mother was t-*ew* famous. Her status was t-*ew* beta. Her burps were t-*ew*—

"Why are you asking *me*?" Derrick chuckled through his nose.

Perfect Storm giggled again, her pitch so snooty that it drew tears from Dylan's eyes like a snake charmer's flute. Even if Derrington didn't like her *that way*, he didn't have to make fun of her. And Perfect Storm didn't have to twirl a cheap nail-file key chain around her finger like she was—

Ehmaga—

"That's the key chain we bought at the dollar store!" she screeched, even though she meant to ask.

"Yup." He grin-nodded.

"Hi, I'm Sammi." She offered her delicate right hand.

"Hey." Dylan shook, giggling away her anxiety.

"Thanks for the sixteen presents." She dangled her nail-file key chain, proudly displaying the key to her new Mini Cooper. "It was such a cute idea, the first thing I asked him was who thought of it."

Derrington confirmed that with a nod.

"And what did he say?" Dylan leaned closer to Sammi, overcome with the urge to lip-kiss her in an "I'm beyond excited you're related to him and not a potential threat" sort of way. But she managed to restrain herself from all physical contact.

"He said . . . " She side-glanced at her brother, warning him she was about to say something dangerous.

Dylan's heart revved again, from joy to heart attack in 1.5 seconds.

"Don't!" Derrington limped toward Sammi.

"What?" Dylan asked, pressing her palm into his red hoodie, holding him back.

Sammi smiled slyly. "He said his future girlfriend helped him."

"Did *not!*" Derrick whipped an empty cup of soda at his sister's head.

She cackle-dodged it by an inch. "Hey, be in the parking lot in three minutes unless you want to hobble home," she warned. "Oh, and nice meeting you, *future girlfriend!*"

"Go!" Derrick lifted a bag of popcorn, but Sammi bolted before he could throw it.

Now that they were suddenly alone, Sammi's confession enveloped them like a thick fart. It was too embarrassing to admit they could smell it but too pungent to pretend it wasn't there. Awkwardly, Dylan and Derrick looked at their feet and cracked up, like a bag of almost thrown popcorn was high-rolling comedy.

The crowd was beginning to thin. Soon the photographers would be gone and Massie would see them.

"Is it true?"

"What?" Derrington asked, even though he knew.

"That I'm your *future girlfriend*?" Dylan's moccasins jingled while she shifted nervously. *OMG, did I seriously just say that?*

"No," he said softly.

The bells stopped. Everything stopped.

"Whaddaya mean?" Dylan squinted, trying to look confused instead of crushed.

"You're my *current* girlfriend." Derrick playfully socked her on the arm.

Dylan smile-sighed, exhaling thirteen years of insecurity.

"Is that okay?"

On the field, Massie was posing for cell phone pictures with a bunch of seventh-graders. It was now or never.

Dylan dared herself to look into Derrick's brown eyes. Double-dared herself to step toward him. And triple-dawg-dared herself to lean in and lip-kiss him.

As if he could read her mind, Derrick stuck his neck out like a rooster and pecked her on the mouth. It was quick. And their mouths were closed. But her heart leapt into her throat and beat like a victory drum. She'd done it! *They'd* done it! If Crush had been the name of a video game, Dylan would just have scored and moved up a level.

Derrick limp-turned halfway around and wiggled his butt with glee.

Did he do that after he kissed Massie? Or was that custom-made just for me?

OMG! MASSIE!!!!!!

Thankfully, the alpha was wrapping up her last cell photo session and hadn't seen a thing.

But someone else had.

Alicia was grinning with satisfaction, waving her phone like a sinister comic book villain.

"Ehmagawd!" Dylan checked her messages, her heart now beating a funeral dirge.

"What *is* it?" Derrick asked with sincerity, like only a new boyfriend can.

"Nothing," Dylan mumbled, nervously clicking the photo Alicia had sent. An image of their lip-kiss popped onto the screen with a message that said "1000 gossip points for me!"

"She *can't*," Dylan gasped, searching the field with wet-eyed urgency.

But Alicia was already gone.

For the first time ever, Massie's white- and purple-accented bedroom smelled like Cinnabon. And nawt the scented candle version from Target. The real, honest-to-goodness, butter-and-sugar, bought-it-at-the-mall, diabetics-beware, jeans-don't-fit, I'll-start-my-diet-on-Monday deal. Yet none of her sleepover guests noticed. Not even Dylan. They all seemed distant, pre-occupied. It was like hearts were the new stomachs.

A buzzing cell phone forced their thoughts back to the room.

"It's mine." Massie tapped her iPhone, basking in the delicious warmth of all eyes on her. "Ehma-y*ay*!" she shrieked. "Dempsey just invited us to Rye Playland Sunday. His parents rented it out for some orphans thing and they have extra tickets."

"Are any other boys going?" Alicia smoothed her ivory, down-filled sleeping bag.

"He invited the Socc-Hers and the Socc-*Hims*." Massie giggled at her little joke.

"Yayyyy!" Claire and Alicia jumped up on the bed and hug-jumped for joy.

"Josh!" Alicia shouted.

"And Cam!" Claire joined in.

"Josh!"

"And Cam!"

"Josh!"

"And Cam!"

"Down!" Massie snapped her fingers, a gesture usually reserved for Bean. "Kris, want me to ask if you can bring Dune even though he's not on the team?"

"Yeah, sure." Kristen rolled onto her tummy, propping her chin on her fists. "Sure."

"Don't sound too excited," Massie mumbled, her thumbs speed-scuttling across her touch screen.

"Whaddaya mean? I sounded excited, didn't I? Because I am. I toe-dally am—"

"So, what's it like having Dune back?" Dylan asked.

Massie rolled her eyes. She had been waiting for the right moment to discuss Dempsey and whether his text meant he liked her, but now Dylan had hijacked the conversation and driven it back to Boringtown.

"Ah-mazing." Kristen nodded excitedly, her head making up for the lack of enthusiasm in her voice.

"Have you guys lip-kissed yet?"

"We haven't been able to cuz I'm grounded."

"You know what?" Alicia sat down on Kristen's butt. "Josh and I wore the same Ralph shirt this week by total accident."

"Apple C." Claire giggled.

"Point!" Alicia lifted her finger just as Kristen bucked Alicia off her butt. Alicia landed on Dylan's leopard-print sleeping bag with a thud.

Dylan quickly turned away.

"Speaking of C"—Alicia sat up and finger-combed her glossy hair—"D, are you still a C-minus, or have you found someone?"

Dylan's eyes narrowed slightly as she folded her arms across her chest.

"C-minus," she blurted, her eyes narrowing even more. "So, um, Kuh-laire, how many times did you and Cam lip-kiss this week?"

Claire blushed. "I don't lip-kiss and tell." She playfully slugged Dylan with her pillow. Then she held up two fingers and giggled.

"*Ehmagawd!*" the girls squealed.

Massie rolled her eyes.

"Dempsey and I will probably lip-kiss after Rye Playland," she interjected, sounding more certain than hopeful. "The only reason we haven't done it already is 'cause he's been so busy with soccer and I've been so busy with—" She suddenly stopped herself. Claire and Cam were in the same situation and *they* still managed to see each other. "Who's ready for my new game?"

"Meeee!" Everyone raised their hands.

"Sit in a circle," Massie instructed.

The girls shimmied onto their sleeping bags and crossed their legs, their satin pj-covered knees touching, in a "we're best friends" sort of way.

"Make room," Massie grunted as she lowered a silver platter of Cinnabons and a crystal bowl of low-fat, low-sodium popcorn into the middle. She pulled Bean onto her lap and joined them.

"This game is called Given/Nawt Given," the alpha announced. "I invented it last night."

"Point?" Alicia asked, sounding bored, like someone who had never invented a game but wished she had.

It's really just a veiled tactic; a way for me to gossip about my crush issues without coming off like an insecure LBR, Massie thought, but she'd sooner have gone bald than admit it.

"The *point* is, we take turns asking each other questions. If your answer is *given,* you get to eat the low-fat popcorn and stay thin. But if it's *nawt given* you have to eat Cinnabon and get opposite of thin."

"Shouldn't it be the other way around?" Claire asked. "You know, like the *reward* is the Cinnabon and the *punishment* is popcorn?"

"Ah-greed." Dylan giggle-high-fived Claire.

"Nawt unless you wanna be the Fat in the Hat on Halloween." Massie rolled her eyes. "Now let's start."

"Pause." Alicia held up her palm. "If our answer is yes, we say 'given' and eat Cinnabon?"

"No, *low-fat popcorn,*" Massie insisted. "Watch. I'll start." She twirled her purple hair streak. "I have a crush."

The girls stared at her blankly.

"Well?" The alpha widened her eyes.

They kept staring.

"Do you have a crush or nawt?" she insisted, exasperated. Did she have to spell everything out for them?

They nodded yes.

"Then say 'given' and eat *popcorn*!"

"Ohhhhh." They giggle-reached for the crystal bowl.

"Hey, Dylan," Alicia purred. "Is there something you'd like to share with everyone?"

"Huh?" Dylan mumbled, her mouth full of popcorn.

"You're a C-plus?" Massie could hear the disappointment in her own voice. How dare Dylan have a crush and not tell the alpha first?

"Ooops!" Dylan regurgitated the chewed corn into a white cloth napkin. Then, rocking onto her knees, she reached for the silver platter. "I got confused." She bit into the round pastry and speed-chewed.

"I bet you did." Alicia lifted her dark arched eyebrows.

"Next." Massie looked to her left.

"'Kay." Claire giggled, already digging into the bowl. "My crush likes me back."

"Given." Alicia joyfully placed a single piece of popcorn on her tongue.

"Given." Kristen did the same.

"Nawt given." Dylan stuffed the rest of the Cinnabon in her mouth.

Massie's hand hovered tentatively above the snacks. Did she look as lame as she felt?

Smugly, Alicia ate another piece of popcorn just to prove she had no doubt.

Dylan swallowed loudly. "I say it's a given."

"How do you know?" Alicia asked, braiding her own hair.

"Because who wouldn't like *her*?" Dylan leaned across the circle and tapped Massie's foot encouragingly, as if she were some spastic boy in Little League. "Soon Massie and Dempsey will be a total couple, and she'll throw water on Derrington, and—"

"I have another one," Massie said, getting to the heart of the matter. "Some guys think Layne's cute. Given or nawt given?"

Claire tentatively took a burnt kernel of popcorn and placed it on her tongue. Of course, if Massie had been playing truthfully she would have too. But come awn, she'd invented this game to *get* answers, nawt give them.

"Nawt given," the other girls replied, reaching for the Cinnabons.

"I've lip-kissed my crush," Alicia blurted. "*Given*. When I got back from Spain."

"Given," Claire blurted proudly.

"Nawt given," Kristen admitted.

"Nawt given." Massie sighed.

"Nawt given," Dylan hissed.

"I am *nawt* lying," Alicia tried again.

"Huh?" Massie blurted, wondering what she was missing but sensing it was something.

Dylan's fists clenched. "I do nawt want to be captain of the Socc-Hers."

"One at a time!" Massie insisted.

Alicia gasped. "I have a crush on my BFFWC's ex!"

"*Pause!*" Massie snapped, suspecting some other force was

at play. She eyed her friends slowly, waiting for one of them to sweat, or cry, or—

"Wait a minute!" Massie's heart fluttered like it did when she was right. "I cannawt believe I didn't pick up on this!" She duck-duck-goose-stepped around the friendship circle, lightly tapping each girl on the head. "I. Have. A. Crush. On." She stopped behind Dylan.

"What?" the redhead screeched.

Massie paused for another second, just to make her sweat. And then: "Chris Abeley!"

Dylan exhaled and proudly bit into a Cinnabon with the rest of the girls.

Hmmm. Really? Massie wondered, slowly padding around the outside of the circle. *Then why the jumpiness?* She steeled herself, perking up her senses like a hunted animal in the wild. Something dangerous was creeping up on her. But *what?* All she could do was hide and wait.

"I heard *Derrington* has a new crush," Alicia announced, and then ate popcorn.

Massie's stomach lurched.

"Aaaaaaand the girl likes him back," Alicia said. She took another handful.

The sickly sweet taste of Cinnabon began creeping up the back of Massie's throat. "Source?" she asked evenly.

"Josh. He saw them kissing."

"Who is it?" Massie stopped pacing, but turned away from her friends to avoid their eyes. The only thing worse than humiliation was pity.

"He won't tell me," Alicia replied. "But I know I can get it out of him if I really want to."

"If I don't find out first," Massie hissed through clenched teeth.

"What are you going to do?" Dylan twisted a clump of hair tightly around her finger.

"I'll start by putting Krazy Glue in her lip gloss."

The girls giggled. Alicia cracked up. Dylan gulped.

"Everyone knows I marked him. Who would do that?" Massie reached for a Cinnabon and took an angry bite.

"Wait." Claire lifted her hand like she was in class. "Was that a question?"

"No," Massie snapped. "This game is over."

CURRENT STATE OF THE UNION	
IN	**OUT**
Find-Her & Kill-Her	Socc-Her

'Nuff said.

Kristen shot up from the floor of the Blocks' Range Rover and slumped down on the tan leather seat. She unzipped her slim-fit black hoodie dress, revealing the top of a red-and-white striped tank. "Sporty, yet sophisticated, right?"

"Bravo." Massie golf-clapped. "The House of H&M has done it again."

Kristen's smile faded. How did she always know?

"Just rate me, okay?"

Each girl held up eight fingers.

"Not bad for H&M." Kristen balled up her mom-approved "I'll be at the library all day studying" sweats and stuffed them in her READING IS FUNDAMENTAL tote.

"Can we *puh-lease* get out of the car now?" Alicia smoothed her too-fancy-for-an-amusement-park emerald green off-the-shoulder satin blouse. "We've been in the back of this lot for fifteen minutes." She crossed her oil-slicked legs, which looked like two glow sticks thanks to a pair of dark denim short shorts.

"Yeah, I have to pee." Dylan squirmed.

"And I told Cam we were here." Claire pressed one of the pen-drawn hearts on her red Converse. "What if—"

"What if *what*, Kuh-laire?" Massie lowered her white

Ray-Bans. "What if Cam has to live without you for a few minutes? What if you have to hang out with your friends a little longer? What if—"

"What if Dempsey goes inside without us and we can't get *in*!" Claire snapped.

Massie consulted the clock on her iPhone. "Okay, Isaac," she called to her driver. "Let's move."

He dropped them at the park's entrance where, thankfully, the Tomahawks, Dune, Layne, Twizzler, and McNugget were still waiting.

"Perfectly late." Massie stepped out of the Range Rover, more than pleased with herself.

"Heyyy," Dempsey wave-called, looking confidently relaxed in khaki cargo shorts, a long-sleeve hooded vintage FREE NELSON MANDELA tee, and beat-up flip-flops.

Crisp fall air rolled off the Long Island Sound, raising the hair on Kristen's arms. Or was it Dempsey's welcoming smile?

"I wasn't sure if you guys were going to come," he said with a relieved smile.

"Oh no." Massie widened her amber eyes. "Were you waiting long?"

In the background, Layne whispered something to Dune and he chuckled. Kristen's insides warmed. Dune and her secret BFF were getting along! But the warmth quickly turned to longing. And then anger. Why couldn't the Pretty Committee be that accepting of Layne? Why did she have to hide their friendship? And why wasn't she more excited to see

Dune? Was it because she knew he wouldn't like her friends? Or was it something else?

"Ready?" Dempsey called, fanning out a stack of free-admission coupons.

"Yeaaaah!" everyone shouted.

He led the group though the turnstiles, fist-pounding the fish-scented breeze.

Massie and Layne scurried to the front, each jockeying to secure a place beside him.

"Ooof!" Layne stopped suddenly, the metal bar cutting across the top of her super-high-waisted yellow jeans.

"Y'okay?" Kristen mumbled into the back of Layne's head.

Layne nodded, her flushed cheeks fading back to pale.

She was grateful Layne tolerated their secret friendship and even more grateful that she believed it was solely to preserve the Witty Committee, rather than the real reason: to preserve Kristen's popularity.

"Dude, the log flume!" Cam smacked Claire playfully on the arm once they were inside the park.

"Owie!" Claire smacked him back. Seconds later they were engaged in a nauseatingly adorable fake fight that made everyone around them want to beat them up for real.

"Yeah!" Josh Hotz pushed back the brim of his navy New York Yankees cap. "Ready to get soaked?" He knocked Alicia's pink cap off her head.

"I am, but my blouse isn't." She pinched the silk.

"Wear this." Josh unzipped his black-and-white checked Billabong hoodie and tossed it to her.

Alicia sniffed the sleeve. "Polo Double Black! I heart that."

Cam pulled the foursome toward the ride, leaving the others to choke on their love dust.

"Look, a caricature artist!" Twizzler shout-pointed at a crusty old man in a blue beret. "Who wants to do it? We can use the drawings for our yearbook pictures." He giggle-snorted.

McNugget and a few of the LBR soccer players raced to his side.

"Layne, you coming?" he called.

Layne looked at Dempsey, whose flip-flops were planted firmly on the gum-stained pavement.

"Nah," she answered. "I'll probably go for something in oils."

"First one there goes first!" Twizzler called. Instantly, he and his gang took off for the splintering easel.

"His yearbook picture is going to look like a thin piece of licorice," Massie joked.

Everyone laughed except Dune and Layne.

"Who wants to try Super Flight?" Derrington asked. "It drops to zero gravity and you experience weightlessness."

"Weightlessness?" Dylan pressed her glossy lips into a sticky puff of cotton candy that she'd just bought. "Sounds good to me," she said, a pink feathery beard dangling from her chin.

"Let's go!" Derrington shouted, speed-limping away before anyone had a chance to respond. Oddly, Dylan was the only one who followed.

"Who wants to try the Dragon Coaster?" Dempsey called.

"Me!" Massie and Layne called at the same time. In a show of support, Kristen and Dune joined them.

Crisp wind blew off the Sound, stinging Kristen's cheeks and tornadoing loneliness through her heart. Bitter cold days and dark afternoons were right around the corner, and with them always came the hollow feeling of emptiness. She lifted her hood and then smiled at Dune. Maybe this winter would be different.

"I can't believe she calls that guy a *Twizzler*!" he whispered.

"Who?" Kristen asked even though she knew.

Dune lifted his chin, gesturing toward Massie, who was up ahead with Dempsey and Layne. "Why is she so mean?"

Kristen debated giving one of the following explanations:

A) She thinks it's funny.
B) She feels better about herself when she puts other people down.
C) Puh-lease! She wasn't serious. Where's your sense of humor?
D) Get used to it.
E) Why do you hate her so much? Gawd! Can't you just stop being so judgmental and right all the time and just have some fun?!!!

But all Kristen said was, "I'll show you *mean*. Last one to the white fence outside the Dragon Coaster rides alone!"

Everyone took off in a mad dash. Sounds of tromping feet

and giggle-gasping circled Kristen's head like a space helmet. Still, anything was better than hearing her own thoughts. Because on her first day out after being grounded, Kristen didn't want to think about her crush not liking her best friend. That kind of stress was easier to deal with during the week, when her mind was tweezer-sharp. Today all she wanted was stomach butterflies and a little weakness in the knees. And if she had to run to get them, then so be it.

"First!" Kristen whacked the sign.

"Second!" Dune shout-panted. Whoever finished after him didn't matter. Massie was no longer their topic of conversation. And that was all she wanted.

"I guess this means we're sitting together." Dune smiled shyly as the rest of their friends ran up behind them.

Kristen slid the shark tooth across its leather strap, tilted her head, and nodded yes.

"You know"—Dune flicked the necklace—"I've never let anyone else wear that."

"Really?" Kristen grinned, waiting to feel that dipping-roller-coaster feeling in her stomach. Only it didn't come. The snaking dragon car hissed to a stop on the wooden track. Everyone raced for the front. Dempsey was in the lead until Layne pushed past Massie and grabbed the hood of his FREE NELSON MANDELA tee, stop-choking him in his path.

"What are you doing?" He pulled the cotton noose away from his thyroid.

"Um, did you drop this?" She held out a crushed box of raisins.

"No." Dempsey coughed. "I think it's yours." He pointed at the black pruney swag wedged between her incisors.

"Oh." Layne picked it out with the corner of the box. "You're right." She squeezed into the car beside him. But before she could sit, Massie yanked her out.

"'Scuse me, Layne, are you a fisherman?"

"No, *why*?"

"Then why are you cutting the line?" She sat down beside Dempsey and lowered the black padded bar.

"Did you see that?" Kristen gasped from a few cars back.

"What?" Dune ran a hand through his matted long hair.

"Nothing," mumbled Kristen, unsure whether she was reacting to Massie's victory or Layne's defeat—or simply the realization that no matter how this ended someone was going to be devastated.

"You stole my seat!" Layne shouted, looking around for some sort of authority figure. But the person in charge was an eighteen-year-old boy with an eyebrow piercing, a shaved head, and a tattoo of Barack Obama on the back of his skull. A thick layer of stubble covered the president, making him look like a pubescent werewolf.

"Take the car behind them," the boy mumble-guided Layne into the available seat. "Any singles want to ride with her?"

Everyone on line shook their heads no.

"That's not fair! She stole my seat!"

The guy lowered the bar over her flailing arms and moved on.

Layne kicked the back of Massie's seat. "You are sooo dead!"

But the alpha giggled at Dempsey, refusing to acknowledge her.

Layne hate-tossed her raisins at the back of Massie's head. "Fine with me!" She pulled a falafel sandwich out of her SUNSHINE TOURS tote and jammed it in her mouth like a competitive eater. "Enjoy the ride!" She speed-chewed.

"You think he knows they're fighting over him?" Kristen whispered to Dune.

"If he does, he's playing it super cool."

Kristen settled into her seat with a satisfied smile. She could tell Dune anything. And if that wasn't the sign of a good crush, she didn't know what was.

With a sudden jerk, the car creaked into motion like an old man getting up to lower the volume on his antiquated television. Still, the people in the back screamed anyway. As the train climbed the tracks to the first hill, Kristen's head fell against the back of her seat—not so much from the gravitational pull as the anxiety weighting down her brain. When they careened down the hill, would Dune . . .

A) Hold her hand?
B) Offer a protective hug?
C) A & B?

or . . .

D) Smack her on the arm like a surf buddy and shout, "Stand up!" ✓

"*What?*" Kristen shouted back, not wanting to believe it.

"Stand up!" Dune gripped her elbow and lifted Kristen into a squat.

"I don't want toooooooooooooooo!" she yelled as they shot down at stomach-roiling speed.

"Ahhhhhhhhh!" everyone shrieked.

Kristen fought to keep her balance in a position usually used for pooing outdoors.

Like Leo on the bow of the *Titanic,* Dune's hair was blowing and his arms were wide, embracing all of nature's goodness in this moment meant just for him. "Riiiiiiide it!"

Three cars ahead, Dempsey's arms were wrapped around Massie, and her face was buried in his chest. A sudden shock of jealousy bolted through Kristen. She wished Dune would put his arm around her like that, instead of making her crouch-stand next to him. For a second she imagined herself leaping from head to head, car to car, like a frog in a lily pond until she got close enough to tear them apart. But why? Was she that sympathetic toward Layne? That able to *feel* the heartache of the people she loved? Compassionate to a dangerous degree? Kristen was about to check on Layne when everything went dark. The car shot into a tunnel, amplifying their screams and distorting their senses. Was this how blind kids felt on Halloween?

"Whooo-hooooo!" Dune finally let go of his grip, allowing Kristen to fall back in her seat and massage her burning quads.

All of a sudden, a giant hand of sunshine smacked her in

the eyes. The car was back outside, soaring and sinking over a series of mini-hills.

Up ahead, Layne was leaning forward, straining her head as if trying to tell Massie a secret.

And then, like an unplugged fire hydrant, a rush of bile-soaked falafel sprayed from her mouth.

Massie slumped forward like a hunchback, too disgusted to move. Finally, she tried to turn around, but the car whipped around the tracks so forcefully she got slammed against the side. Dempsey managed to ask Layne if she was okay. She replied with an enthusiastic head-nod and two thumbs-up.

Kristen smacked Dune's leg repeatedly, trying to show him the spectacle. But he was standing again, and didn't seem to notice.

Finally, the car click-clacked to a stop and everyone stopped screaming, except Massie.

"I am so suing you!" She peeled off her ivory, now-falafel-flavored cashmere cardigan and whipped it onto the track.

"Sorry." Layne grimaced. "I just feel-*afel*."

"Here." Dempsey handed Layne his canteen without the slightest concern for puke-chunk backwash.

"Keep that LBR away from me," Massie hissed in Kristen's ear as they stepped onto the wooden platform.

"*Me?*" Kristen asked feeling slightly wobbly. "How am I—"

"*Nike!*" Massie insisted.

"Huh?"

"Just *do* it!" she hissed.

The deck shook with the stampede of new people rushing to claim their seats.

"What am I supposed to *do* with her?"

"I dunno." Massie stomped her foot. "Just think of—"

"See ya!" Layne shouted from the back of the dragon's tail. She and Dempsey were seated thigh to thigh as a padded bar lowered across their chests.

"Hey, that's not fair!" Massie made her way toward them.

The pierced guy stopped her with the handle of his mop. "There's a line!"

"Well, *she* didn't wait in it!"

He lowered the wood lever, starting the ride. "Pukers coast again. Plus one." He shrugged. "Park policy."

"Well, what do *I* get?"

"Whaddaya want?" He raised his pierced eyebrow, implying himself.

"*Ew*, nawt *that*." Massie turned on her heel.

"There's gotta be something I can do to make you feel better." He rubbed his stubbly head.

"It's too late, thanks to *her*." She pointed at Kristen and then stormed off.

Kristen stood on the platform, stiff with shock. *How had this become her fault?* She could feel Dune's eyes on her. Waiting for her to speak? Searching for something to say? Plotting Massie's demise?

The car rolled back into the loading area.

"Awwww, you waited for us?" Layne gushed, as Dempsey unwrapped himself from her protective hold.

Kristen tried to smile, her mouth twitching like a dying worm.

"What's wrong?" Dempsey lifted the bar and stepped onto the platform. He placed a warm hand on her shoulder. "You look like you lost your best friend."

"She did," Dune chuckled with amusement. But Kristen failed to see the humor. In fact, she failed to see anything. Her vision blurred instantly with tears.

Dylan sniffed her arm.

Faint traces of Derrick's sweatshirt—or rather, his spicy deodorant—lingered on her skin like fine French parfum. She wanted to sniff it all night but paced herself, fearing each inhalation would suck the smell from her pores, like a Dust-Buster on shag, until the scented crumbs were gone.

Lifting a cobalt blue velvet throw pillow off her gray chaise, she buried her arm for the same reason her mother would lock up the Dove chocolates: to avoid temptation. Then she gazed up at her peach-colored ceiling as if it were a flat-screen TV, replaying every perfect detail of her perfect day at Rye Playland. How she and Derrick had managed to lose the group the minute they'd gotten there. *Oops!* And how they'd laughed their way to stronger abs. And fed each other snacks like Siamese twins joined at the mouth. They'd even ridden every ride—twice! And they'd done it all without seeing Massie.

Ding.

Dylan felt like a lamp that had just gotten plugged in. The text was from *him*. She could just tell.

Derrick: Wanna double to SKL 2morrow?

Dylan bicycled her bare feet in the air. And then she turned him down.

Dylan: Can't ☹
Derrick: Lunch @ the trailers?

Her fingers practically cramped in protest.

Dylan: Can't ☹
Derrick: Study?

Dylan hit send on another sad face.
Her heart pounded, waiting for him to respond.

Derrick: Didn't u have fun today?

Dylan's heart felt like an obese person trying to jump.

Dylan: Given.
Derrick: Then?????

Dylan quickly unfastened the clasp on her gold chain necklace and slid off her diamond *D* charm.
Rock side up, I tell him the truth. Rock side down, I lie.
She took a deep breath. With the flick of her thumb Dylan launched the charm above her. It landed on her chaise with a muted thud.
Diamond side up.

Dylan: Truth?

Derrick: Y

Dylan: U still belong 2 MB

Derrick: Belong?????????

Dylan shook her head while she typed, finding it hard to believe she was going to reveal one of Massie's secret rituals. And even harder to believe she was honoring it.

Dylan: She sprayed u w/Chanel No 19. That means she has a hold on u.

Derrick: Nsane!

Dylan: Not 2 her. Can't violate or IL be out of the PC. Only way 2 break it is if she throws h2o on you.

Derrick: Tell her 2 do it.

Dylan: Can only do it when shez ready.

Derrick: So can u hang out?

Dylan: Not legally.

There was no screen activity for at least twenty seconds. And Dylan was certain she had lost him for good this time. Until . . .

Derrick: 1 Solution, 9 Letters.

After a solid minute of serious brain activity, Dylan finally figured it out.

Dylan: ☺

One word . . . nine letters . . . two ah-dorable.

Detention.

It was so juh-eeen-yus. All Dylan and Derrick had to do was get in trouble every day. Then they could be together from three thirty to four thirty in the afternoon, Monday through Friday. They'd be *après*-school soul mates. Detention Daters. Incarcerated Crushes. And they would stay that way until Massie released Derrington and gave them her blessing. Which was bound to happen . . . eventually.

The plan was set. The crime was simple. The time was now.

First period was over and the halls were rife with slamming lockers, hushed gossip exchanges, and speed-gloss sessions. But no one dared talk on cell phones. Because "nonemergency mobile use" was strictly forbidden between classes. And anyone caught using would get an immediate detention.

No.

Questions.

Asked.

Derrick was positioned outside Principal Burns's office when Dylan arrived. As discussed, they were dressed in black, sending a message to the authorities that they were rebels.

Their eyes met, a flicker of acknowledgment passing between them like CIA operatives on assignment.

As usual, the frosted glass door of Principal Burns's office clicked open at 9:28 a.m. Out she bounded, en route to her weekly board meeting, her gangly body coasting among the students like a giraffe through a herd of gazelle, her gray bob holding firm despite her long, breezy steps.

Students slowed, letting her pass, like drivers making room for a wailing ambulance.

Derrick nodded once.

Without a moment's hesitation, he lifted his black and green Sidekick, leaned against a locker, and began shout-talking like he was standing by the speakers at a Megadeth concert.

"You serious, man?" he yelled, examining his cuticles. "'Cause he told me seven goals in one game was the record. And now you're telling me it's nine?" He paused. "Show me proof, goof!" He paused and then burst out laughing.

Principal Burns hurried toward Derrick, wagging her finger. Dylan quickly pulled out her cell phone, but her palms were slick with stress-sweat, and it crashed to the floor. The battery slid one way and the phone slid the other. By the time she had everything back together it was too late. Principal Burns had grabbed the Sidekick out of Derrick's hand and given him two detentions. One for having a nonemergency conversation, and the other for being in the main building when he was a trailer student.

One word. Nine letters.

Backfired.

Determined to start detention-dating as soon as possible, Dylan and Derrick tried a new tack the morning after he had finished his two detentions.

Using the standard "bad sushi" excuse, Dylan broke away from the Pretty Committee and raced toward the bathrooms. And then she snuck out back and scrambled over to Pigeon Parking Lot, where she and Derrick had an early morning date with two bags of birdseed and a hungry flock of fowl.

They greeted each other with giggle-high-fives and hopeful smiles that refused to settle, as if nailed in place.

First period would begin in three minutes. Which meant Ms. Dunkel, the overflow trailer teacher, would be making her way across PPL in one minute and thirty seconds.

Dylan ripped open the plastic bag with her teeth. "Ready?" Seeds spilled into her mouth, and she immediately spit them to the asphalt. A week ago she would have worried that Derrick might find the seed-spit a turnoff, but not anymore. She knew he'd laugh. And he did.

"Ew, sorry." Dylan wiped her tongue on the sleeve of her gray cashmere waffle-weave sweater dress.

He dumped a bunch of seeds in his mouth and shot them

like bullets from an AK-47. "No problem." He grinned playfully.

As if cued by Alfred Hitchcock himself, a flock of pigeons swarmed the lot and landed at their feet.

"Ahhhhhh!" Dylan dropped her bag and ran for a nearby tree.

Derrick did the same, with a limp, but without the high, shrieking scream.

They giggle-watched as dozens of pigeons poked the pavement liked winged jackhammers.

"Ehmagawd, there she is!" Dylan pointed at Ms. Dunkel, who was parking her red Subaru Forester while gray feathers drifted to the ground amid the feeding frenzy.

"Come on." Derrick tugged her arm. "We need to get out there and take responsibility for this."

"Shouldn't we wait until it calms down a little?" Dylan dug her nails into the tree trunk. "We could get hepatitis or something."

"No!" He tugged. "We need to—"

"Scram, rats!" Strawberry appeared in the parking lot, waving her arms at the cooing surge.

"Ahhhhh! How are we going to get to the trailers?" yelled Kori, her LBRBFF. "Throw something at them!"

They removed their backpacks and whipped them onto the ground like they were in flames. Three rattled pigeons flapped their wings and rose a few inches, but landed almost immediately. The rest kept pecking.

Suddenly, more came.

They hovered just above the girls' heads, looking for their point of entry, while dropping poop and shedding feathers.

"What do they *want*?" Kori cried.

"Food!" Strawberry scooped up their packs. "Give them food."

Kori whimpered as she unzipped her polka-dot LeSportsac. "Low-fat organic cheese or Tofurky?"

"Both!" Strawberry shouted. "Whatever!" She whipped a Fuji apple into the chaos like a grenade.

Derrick and Dylan shook with silent laughter.

"What is going *on* here?" Ms. Dunkel yelled.

The pigeons scattered at once.

"Feeding the pigeons is against school policy," she insisted, paying no mind to their tear-soaked faces.

"But we weren't—"

"Detentions for both of you!" Ms. Dunkel grabbed their arms and yanked them toward the trailers. "I hope you like washing cars."

"No fair!" cried Strawberry as she and Kori scrambled to keep up with their irate teacher.

"No fair!" Dylan stomped her red ankle boot.

"I better go too or I'll get another detention without you." Derrick waved, hobbling backward.

"What do we do now?" Dylan pouted.

"We'll go for plan C at lunch."

"'Kay." Dylan beamed. Despite her disappointment, she was still smiling. This was the most fun she'd ever had staying out of trouble.

Dylan knocked organic turkey meatballs from one side of her plate to the other.

"It's lunch, nawt an abacus," Massie teased.

"Point!" Alicia giggle-lifted her finger in the air.

"I'm not hungry," Dylan lied. She had better plans for the balls.

"Neither is Kristen." Massie checked the time on her iPhone. "This is the third day she's skipped lunch because of soccer captain stuff." She made air quotes when she said "soccer captain stuff." "But she can't hide forever. Eventually she's gonna have to explain why she just stood there while Layne rode off with my crush at—"

A chunk of firm tofu smacked Massie on the forehead.

Uh-oh. Wrong forehead.

"What the—?"

Everyone stopped eating and turned. But no one dared laugh. Not when the BOCD alpha had bean curd all over her T-zone.

"Sucka!" Derrington shouted . . . and then his face blanched. "Ooops. Sorry, Massie," he apologized, although he was looking straight at Dylan.

Massie rose out of her seat, her bottom teeth bared like

a bulldog's. "Gawd, will you puh-lease stop flirting with me? It's pathetic times ten." She pinched the side of Dylan's tray, casually dragging it toward her. "I've moved awn, okay?"

All eyes were on her, and, like a true alpha, she refused to let all that attention go to waste.

"Hey, maybe if you had a pair of these you'd be able to get over me." Massie lifted two of Dylan's turkey balls and hurled them at his head.

"A direct hit!" Massie high-fived herself as they bounced off his chest, leaving a saucy skid mark above the alligator on his white Lacoste.

The Pretty Committee scurried under their bamboo table for cover.

"Massie! Massie! Massie!" chanted the surrounding wannabes.

"Save your Trina Turk tunic!" Dylan urged Massie. "Hide. Let me get him."

Dylan fired at her crush like a machine in a batting cage, nailing her target with every toss.

"Oof! Ow! Ugh!" Derrington shouted after each ball made contact. "Take that!" he bellowed, returning fistfuls of tofu cubes.

"Dylan! Dylan! Dylan!"

"Save your waffle dress," Massie begged Dylan. "I'll finish him off." Before Dylan could stop her, Massie had climbed up on her chair, redirecting everyone's attention back to her.

"No, I'll do it!" Dylan whipped another meatball.

"No, *me*!" Massie whipped two.

"What is going on here?" Principal Burns appeared, shielding herself with a wood tray.

The chanting stopped suddenly.

"Ms. Block, it looks like you're responsible."

"No, I am!" Dylan stepped forward.

"No, I am!" Derrick announced.

"No need to fight about it." Principal Burns grinned smugly. "There are plenty of detentions to go around. I'll see all three of you in here after school with mops." She clapped twice. "Everyone back in their seats. And Mr. Harrington, get back to your trailer!"

Once he was gone, Massie sat with a sigh.

"Gawd." She wiped her face with a cloth napkin. "He really *needs* to get over me."

No, you need to get over yourself! Dylan wanted to scream. Instead she tried another approach. "Maybe if you break the hold it will—"

"Not with this mystery vamp on the loose."

"Why?" Dylan asked in a measured tone, quaking nervously below the surface of her skin.

"Because I don't have a replacement yet. And if he goes public before I do—"

"He's a guy, Massie, nawt a stock."

"Then why are you so desperate for me to *trade*?"

"I'm nawt," Dylan snapped, flicking a chunk of tofu off her hand and sinking into the Great Depression.

Dylan stared at Massie's Evian water as they dragged the heels of their ankle boots down the barren hall toward detention. The water sloshed around innocently as she swung it, forward and back, completely oblivious to its life-altering power.

"I can't believe you turned yourself in." Massie swung open the door to the café. "It's almost like you *wanted* a detention."

Dylan tried to swallow the invisible hair extensions lodged in the back of her throat. "I was standing up for *you*," she managed. "I didn't want you to get punished alone."

"Ohhhhh. That's nice." Massie took a long swig of water.

"Hey." Derrington limped into the café a few seconds later. "Is it clean? Did you finish? Can we go?"

Dylan giggled. Massie rolled her eyes.

The lights were dim, giving the impression that the overworked tables and chairs were taking a much-needed break, and that the long day was over. Only three mops by table eighteen and a sauce-stained floor indicated otherwise.

"Let's get this over with." Massie led the charge.

As if reading Dylan's mind, Derrick zeroed in on Massie's water bottle and lifted his brows suggestively. Before Dylan could stop him, he faked an ankle spasm and bashed into the alpha, knocking the bottle from her hand. Water sloshed everywhere, soaking his PARIS HILTON FOR PRESIDENT T-shirt.

Dylan flashed him a quick "it soooo doesn't work that way" glare.

"Sorry, my bad." He backed away from Massie, waving his hands apologetically.

"Gawd." Massie rolled her eyes with disdain, then turned to Dylan. "Let's just finish so we can get out of here and go to Nunya."

Dylan nodded like she couldn't have agreed more, even though she had no clue where that was.

"What's Nunya?" Derrick asked, slapping a sopping mop on the floor.

"Nunya business!" Massie lifted her palm. Dylan high-fived her like they were still the best of friends.

Which technically they were, right?

Just to be sure, Dylan made it a point not to even glance at Derrington while they cleaned. She whispered with Massie and giggled at her jokes, as if they were alone.

By the time everything was clean, Dylan was certain the alpha had no clue what was really going on. Not even Massie could hide the pain of betrayal that well.

Outside, the sun had started to fade. And so had all hope that Dylan and Derrick would ever get to spend any real time together.

"See ya!" Derrick hopped onto his black bike and pedaled off, not bothering to wait for a response.

"You think he's going to meet the new *me*?" Massie asked as they shuffled toward her Range Rover.

Dylan's stomach lurched at the thought. "Maybe."

Massie cocked her head and looked at the mud-colored sky, considering something. "You've been spending a lot of time with him lately—"

All breathing stopped. This was it. The moment that would change everything. Dylan closed her eyes like she was about to get slapped.

"Did he mention anyone to you?"

Dylan exhaled with gale force. "Nope."

Massie laughed lightly to herself. "I'd almost think it was you if he was, you know, into that sort of thing."

"Into *whatsortofthing*?" Dylan heard herself screech.

"You know, triple B's."

"Huh?"

"Big-boned betas." Massie giggled.

Dylan clenched her fists. She was seriously considering violence, when something warm splattered on her head.

Massie burst out laughing.

Without another word, Dylan and her poo-soaked skull ran sobbing toward the bathroom. Because that's what you do after you've been dumped on twice in a matter of seconds.

Massie felt like a chocolate cupcake.

Not because she had on too much self-tanner. Or because her gut was hanging over her Socc-Hers uniform. Actually, it was quite the opposite. She looked ah-mazing. Dozens of cheering fans poked giant foam No. 1 fingers in the air while chanting her name. That was the icing.

But just below the sugary surface was another layer. And it had a completely different texture.

It was dry and crumbly. But mostly bitter. Bitter because Kristen hadn't helped her secure Dempsey. Bitter because Layne might actually have a chance. Bitter because Alicia was a better dancer, and knew it. Bitter because Claire and Cam were the perfect couple. Bitter because Alicia and Josh were running a close second. Bitter because Derrington was moving on. Bitter because her "triple B" comment to Dylan had been triple mean. And bitter because she couldn't bring herself to apologize.

On one level, it was nice knowing she wasn't the only girl on the team with a big fake smile. Dylan was covering her dry, bitter cake with icing too. And knowing that made Massie feel ah-*lot* less pathetic.

Tom-tom. Tom-tom. Tom-ta-ta-tom-tom. Tom-tom. Tom-tom.

Tom-tom. Tom-ta-ta-tom-tom. Tom-tom. Tom-tom. Tom-tom. Tom-ta-ta-tom-tom. Tom-tom.

BOCD's marching band began playing the official tribal drumbeat of the Tomahawks while the teams took the field.

"Socc-Hers, prepare!" Massie lifted her clutch feathers over her head and shook.

The rest of the team followed and began.

"WE DON'T KNOW WHAT'S WRONG OR RIGHT,
ALL WE KNOW IS OUR TEAM'S TIGHT!
WE DON'T CARE WHAT'S OUT OR IN,
JUST AS LONG AS OUR GUYS WIN!
IF IT'S LOSING THAT YOU FEAR,
FRANKLY, WE DON'T GIVE A CHEER!
WHOOOOOOO!"

They ended in a spirited tableau that paid homage to the *High School Musical 3* movie poster. Even the players applauded. Cam smiled just for Claire. Josh smiled for Alicia. Dempsey smiled for one of them. And Derrington, who was sitting in the stands again with Kristen and Dune, smiled for . . . Massie followed his gaze. It led straight to . . .

Ehmaaaaaga—

Someone's bony finger poked her in the ribs.

"Let's *gooooo!*" Alicia hissed. "The game started and you're just standing there. How 'bout we do Score Galore, with the dance sequence from *Stomp the Yard*."

Massie's nostrils flared, wishing she could inhale Alicia

and her cocky know-it-all dancer attitude and sneeze her out into Pigeon Parking Lot, where she would lie in a snotty, bird poo–covered heap until cheerleading season was over.

"We're doing Cleat Feet." Massie turned to her team and shouted, "Ready? And!"

"CLEATS!" (clap-clap) *"ON YOUR FEET!"* (clap-clap)
"SWEAT!" (clap-clap) *"ON THE NET!"* (clap-clap)
"SCORE!" (clap-clap) *"ONE MORE!!!!!!"* (clap-clap)

Derrington pulled himself up onto one leg and wiggled his butt in praise. And then smiled again . . . at *her.*

Dylan—*yes, Dylan*—responded with a flirty ponytail toss and a lower-lip nibble. Normally, Massie would have suspected Derrington's Dylan-smiles were misfires: the result of a lazy eye or an attempt to inspire jealousy. But they *had* been spending a lot of time together. Derrington *was* rumored to be with another girl. And they both thought burps were funny. Annnnnd, come to think of it, Dylan *was* showing a lot of interest in the Chanel No. 19 hold, or rather, its release.

"One more time!" someone shouted.

Alicia!

And the Socc-Hers were doing Cleat Feet again.

"CLEATS!" (clap-clap) *"ON YOUR FEET!"* (clap-clap)

Who did Alicia think she was, calling the cheers?

"SWEAT!" (clap-clap) *"ON THE NET!"* (clap-clap)

Did Derrington really like Dylan? Was *Cosmo* wrong? Did boys like funny girls after all?

"SCORE!" (clap-clap)

Oof! Alicia smashed into Massie.

"ONE MORE!!!!!!" Alicia yelled. And they clap-clapped.

"Watch where you're going!" Massie barked.

"Me?" Alicia barked back. "You've been in a total daze since the game started."

The Socc-Hers slowed down to watch the fight.

"Again!" Massie called.

"Same cheer?" Layne moaned.

"Yeah!" Massie waved her peacock feathers under the LBR's sensitive nose. "And get it right this time. Ready? And!"

"CLEATS!" (clap-clap) *"ON YOUR FEET!"* (clap-clap)

Alicia smashed into Massie again. "Turn left! Nawt right!"

"SWEAT!" (clap-clap) *"ON THE NET!"* (clap-clap)

Massie seethed. "It's right first, then left! Gawd. Just because you took a few amateur dance lessons doesn't make you Julianne Hough." She gave Alicia a shove.

"Opposite of whatever you said!" Alicia shoved her back. "Because I *am* better than you!"

"Are nawt!" Massie fought to catch her balance as Dempsey ran toward them, kicking the ball toward the goal.

"SCORE!" (clap-clap) *"ONE MORE!!!!!!"* (clap-clap)

But the weight of Massie's ponytail threw her off, and she smashed right into Dempsey as he passed. He lost his footing and rolled over on his ankle. A stocky guy in a gold and blue jersey captured the ball, sped off in the other direction, and scored one for the other team.

"Dempsey!" Layne shouted, racing to his side, along with his coaches and his parents.

He groaned through gritted teeth while they peeled off his sock.

"Boooooooooooo!" the crowd began shouting.

"Alicia!" Massie squealed, quickly standing. "I can't believe you pushed me!"

She addressed the crowd. "She pushed me!"

"Opposite of true!" Alicia shouted back.

"Booooooooooo!" the crowd continued, thumbs down, heads shaking in disgust.

"It was an accident!" Massie pleaded while her squad gathered around Dempsey.

They lifted him onto a stretcher and carried him off. Layne and Twizzler scurried after him.

"What are you doing?" Massie called. "The game's not over!" She had considered following Dempsey as well, but they hadn't even lip-kissed yet. It wasn't her place. And if *she* wasn't going, Layne certainly wasn't. "Get back here or you're off the squad."

"Fine," Layne shouted over her shoulder. "I'm off the squad!"

"Twizzler! That goes for you too!"

"She's my partner! We come as a pair." He followed Layne, his entire body burning red.

Massie was so embarrassed, she had no idea what to do next. Spontaneous alien abduction was looking like her only way out.

The crowd began chanting, "Purse . . . purse . . . purse . . . ," while pointing at . . . *her*!

Massie's icy heart melted instantly. *Cancel the aliens!* All was forgiven. They still loved her. They still wanted to be her. They still admired her accessories. Giving them what they wanted, she waved her beautiful custom peacock-feather pom-pom purse in the air and grinned.

". . . purse . . . purse . . . purse . . . ," they chanted even louder.

"Here it is!" She waved her purse harder. "Genuine peacock!"

Alicia tapped her on the shoulder. "Hey, Hilary *Deaf*." She smirked. "They're saying *curse*." She giggled. "Nawt *purse*!"

Massie gasped.

Just then someone threw a giant No. 1 finger at her back. It was made of foam, but it cut like a knife.

Dune *dehhhh*-finitely had lip-kissing on the brain. And spent most of the soccer game talking about it. Particularly how his surfer friends had lip-kissed some local Tavarua girls and how *he* had held back because *he* was saving himself for Kristen. It was everything she dreamed he'd say when she lay in bed night after night, missing him. But come awn! Did he *have* to bring it up right when Carter Alexander was about to score? It was beyond distracting.

Five minutes later, his pinky grazed hers. It was sweet times ten. But weird times twenty. For some reason, her heart didn't race and her palms didn't sweat. But they probably would have if Derrington hadn't been shouting at his team-mates and cursing his ankle for keeping him out of the game, right? It was like trying to concentrate on math problems when Alicia was snapping her gum.

Nine minutes post pinky-graze, Dune began feeding Kristen french fries. It was so romantic two girls sitting behind them actually *awwwwed*. Their jealousy filled Kristen with pride, reminding her how completely ah-dorable her crush was. She vowed, from that moment on, to focus less on the game and more on Dune. But then Massie tripped Dempsey, and Dempsey looked hurt. And they put him on a stretcher.

And took him away. And, well . . . Dune-appreciation had been replaced with Dempsey-concern. And just like that, the *awwwwww* moment was *awwwwwwl* gone.

Still, Dune had invited himself over to Kristen's so they could do their environmental studies homework together, and she'd accepted. He'd ah-bviously try to lip-kiss her while they were working, and maybe *that* would take her mind off Massie, Layne, and Dempsey.

Kristen shook the chatter from her brain and slid her key in the front door lock.

"Hello?" Marsha called from the kitchen.

The condo smelled embarrassingly fishy—like salmon. *Ugh!* Why hadn't she brought Dune on lasagna night? Now he would associate her with that smell forever.

"Krist-mas, is that you?"

Kristen tossed her BFFWC key chain on the front-hall table and then locked the door behind her. "Who else would it be?" She rolled her eyes, letting Dune know the goofy nickname was *soooo* not something she backed.

Dune undulated his hand like a wave: his way of saying "go with the flow." Kristen clenched her fists. Didn't anything ever annoy him?

"Oh, hello." Her mother appeared in the hall wearing mismatched oven mitts and a scowl. "No one mentioned Dune was coming over."

Kristen opened her mouth to respond but Dune beat her to it.

"Yeah, it was kind of a last-minute thing, Mrs. Gregory."

He smiled sweetly. "I need some help with my environmental studies paper and your daughter is the smartest one in the class, so she offered to help."

"How thoughtful." Marsha flashed her I'm-not-buying-it-but-I'll-pretend-to-for-now-and-we'll-talk-about-it-later smile. "Will you be staying for dinner?"

"No," they both answered at the same time, neither one wanting this tension to last any longer than necessary.

"We'll be in my room." Kristen made a break for the hall.

Dune's face lit up like a ringing cell phone.

"The light in the dining room is *much* better," Marsha insisted on her way back to the kitchen, leaving zero room for discussion.

With a defeated sigh, Kristen unwrapped her blue-and-white striped scarf and tossed it by her keys.

"Hey!" Dune examined her neck like a thirsty vampire.

"What?" Kristen shifted uncomfortably, feeling very Bella Swan–ish.

"Where's my shark tooth?"

Kristen's hand rushed to her chest, her fingers spider-crawling around her throat. "I—" Her body flushed with prickling heat. Where was it? How long had it been missing? How could she not have noticed?????

"Did you lose it?"

"What?" Kristen felt her neck again. *"No!"*

Dune folded his arms across his black plaid Billabong hoodie and raised his eyebrows.

"It's, um, in my locker," she managed. "Safe and sound. I took it off for gym. I tried to put it back on after volleyball but I had a brutal hangnail and I couldn't do up the clasp and when I asked for help the bell rang so I—" Someone pounding on the neighbor's door offered a welcome distraction. "Wow." She giggled nervously. "They must *really* want to get inside."

Dune didn't bother responding.

"Don't worry." Kristen undulated her hand like a wave, mimicking his earlier "go with the flow" hand gesture. "I'll get it tomorrow."

He finally smiled. "I better call my dad and tell him I'm here."

Kristen nodded in agreement, anxious for a minute to recover.

While Dune pulled out his cell and paced the parquet hall, she struggled to remember the last time she had the necklace. They'd been at Rye Playland . . . about to ride the Dragon Coaster. . . . Dune had said he'd never let anyone else wear it. . . .

Suddenly the hallway knocker was knocking on *her* door.

Kristen got up on her tiptoes and peeked though the peephole. A giant cellophane-wrapped gift being held by pink sequined gloved hands was all she could see.

Cautiously, Kristen opened the door.

"Layne?"

"Hey." She stepped inside, her face completely distorted by the iridescent plastic.

Kristen rushed to help her set the giant basket on the table. "What *is* all this?" she asked the asphyxiating menagerie of Webkinz and tightly packed Wonka candy.

"A get-well basket for Dempsey," Layne trilled, massaging her cramped arms. "His parents wouldn't let me ride in the ambulance with him so I thought I'd meet them back here." She removed an enormous silver clip-on hoop and pressed her ear against the door. Her narrow green eyes shifted back like she was being hypnotized.

"I hope they're not keeping him overnight for observation."

"He hurt his *ankle*," Kristen snapped, angry with herself for not having gotten him anything.

Layne clipped her hoop back on. "Anyway, is it cool if I hang until he gets back?"

Before Kristen could answer, Layne unzipped her fake-leopard bomber jacket and hung it on the doorknob. "Salmon?" She sniffed.

Kristen lowered her head in her hands. "Is it *that* bad?"

Layne tugged the shark tooth around her neck and nodded yes.

"Ehmagawd, you found it!" Kristen hugged Layne, inhaling her Neutrogena sesame body oil–scented skin. "Give! Give! Give! Before Dune sees it!" She wiggled her fingers as if tickling a baby's chin.

In the dining room, Dune said goodbye to his father, then closed his phone with a victorious snap.

"Oh! Good. He's here." Layne's half-smile spread to full.

Kristen speed-nodded. "Yeah, hurry—give it back before he sees you wearing it," she whispered.

"Are you sure it's yours?" Layne asked casually as Dune shuffled toward them.

"Yeah. Where was it?"

"Under the Dragon Coaster."

Kristen couldn't believe it had been gone for four days and she hadn't noticed.

"Is that *Layne*?" Dune called, sounding pleasantly surprised.

"Hurry, wear *this*." Kristen tossed her striped scarf at Layne's chest.

Layne stepped back, letting it fall to the floor.

"What are you—"

"You'll get the tooth when I get Dempsey."

"Huh?"

"Hey." Dune appeared, grinning.

Layne smiled hello, casually covering her neck.

Was this *seriously* happening?

"What're ya doin' here?" His smile faded, probably because her visit meant he wasn't going to be getting his lip kiss— something he probably should have realized after his run-in with Marsha.

Layne's pink sequin–covered thumb gestured to the gift basket. "Dempsey."

"Ahhhhh." Dune nodded like he completely understood.

"Well, we were just about to study, so if you want to take your jacket and cover up and wait in my room until he gets home, you're more than welcome." Kristen tossed the faux fur at Layne's chest. "It's super cold in there."

"No deal, banana peel." Layne tossed the jacket back.

Another knock on the door interrupted them. Maybe it was Dempsey. Then Layne would leave before Dune noticed the necklace! Kristen once again lifted herself up to the peephole.

A big amber eye stared back.

"*No!*" Kristen gasped. Her knees turned to liquid. Her tongue felt like machine-washed cashmere. Her heart pounded like it was trying to escape.

How would she ever explain why Layne was there?

"Hide!" Kristen ducked, pulling her friends away from the door.

"Who is it?" Dune whispered.

"Kids selling cookies," she blurted, despite her overwhelming lack of saliva.

"We should buy some," Layne blurted. "For Dempsey."

"Can't," Kristen insisted, ignoring the knocking. "Mom hates cookies."

"But—"

"And kids."

The knocking finally stopped. Kristen exhaled, her heart slowing to a jog.

And then the top lock clicked left.

Impossible!

And the bottom lock clicked right.

Just an adrenaline-induced hallucination, right?

"Dad?" Kristen whimpered, hoping it might be her father returning early from his golf trip. And that his left eye had happened to change color while he was gone.

The brass knob jiggled.

"*Baghead?*" Layne whimpered.

And then turned.

"Ahhhh!" Layne scurried behind Dune.

Slowly, the door cracked open, and the suede toe of a jingling moccasin appeared.

"Smells like salmon." Massie winced, smugly pinching a key between her thumb and index finger.

"That answers my first question," Kristen managed, despite her extreme shakiness.

"What's your second one?" Massie dropped the key in her GREEN IS THE NEW BLACK gym tote.

Kristen didn't know where to begin. Questions popped around her brain like kernels in the microwave. Things like:

- How did you get a key to my condo?
- What are you doing here?
- Have you finally stopped blaming me for Layne and Dempsey's ride on the Dragon Coaster?
- Did you realize that their hangout was beyond my control and that you've been giving me the silent treatment all week for *nothing*?
- Can you see Layne hiding behind Dune right now?
- If you do not see Layne hiding behind Dune right now, when *are* you going to see her?
- What will you do to me at that time?
- What excuse will I come up with for having her here?
- Will you believe it?

"Um, Kristen." Massie snapped her fingers. "Are you an astronaut?"

"No, why?" Kristen shook her head like an Etch A Sketch, erasing the chaos in her mind.

"Then why are you spacing?"

"Sorry." Kristen flashed a fake "everything's okay" smile. "Come in."

Massie entered, dragging a clear wheelie over the Gregorys' happy face welcome mat. The suitcase was stuffed with candles, aromatherapy oils, comic books, video games, and the DVD *Bend It Like Beckham*. A big glitter heart said, Humpy Dempsey Had a Great Fall ☺ . . . and It's All Alicia's Fault ☹ in silver metallic marker.

"How did you get a key to my house?" Kristen managed.

"It's *nawt* a house!"

"Real nice." Dune rolled his eyes.

"What? It's *true*." Massie widened her eyes, trying to look innocent. "Anyway, I had Inez make copies during our first sleepover." Massie shrugged as if that were perfectly normal. "In case of emergency."

"What's the 'emergency'?" Kristen made air quotes, her tone more aggressive than usual. But Dune's presence gave her strength. Layne's gave her anxiety. And when mixed together they tasted like anger.

"I wanted to give this to Dempsey when he got back from the hospital." Massie petted her suitcase.

Dune snickered.

"What's *this*?" Massie shrieked at Layne's gift basket. "One-Ew-Hundred-Flowers?" Her top lip curled in disgust as she pinched the cellophane between her fingers like it was sweat-stained polyester.

"Hey!" Layne stepped out from behind Dune. "That's mine!"

"What is *she* doing here?"

Kristen's mouth hung open like a thirsty dog's.

"Ehmagawd." Massie jingle-stomped her moccasin. "Are you helping *her* get Dempsey?"

Kristen tried again. Still, nothing came out.

"Is she *paying* you?" Massie screeched in disbelief.

Kristen searched Layne's face for an appropriate answer.

"Ehmagawd, she *is* paying you," Massie gasped. "Seriously, Kristen, how poor are you?"

Dune gasped in disbelief.

Massie turned to him. "What?"

Don't speak! Don't speak! Don't—

"Why would her *best friend* have to pay her?" he asked innocently.

Nooooooooooooooooooooooooooooooooooooooooooooooooooooooooooooooooooooooooooooooooooooooooooooooooooooooooo!

"I *don't*!" Massie twirled her long ponytail extension. "I was talking about *Layme*."

"So was I," Dune blurted. "They hung out together all summer. And from what I noticed, Kristen has a lot more fun with *Layme* than she does with you, *Assie*!"

"Yeah!" Layne high-fived Dune.

"Really? And how much fun is she having with *you, EW-N?*"

Massie turned to Kristen. Her cheeks were burning red. Her amber eyes were dark. And she was exhaling through her nose like a vengeful dragon. It was like watching a tropical storm gather force. "Is that *true*?"

Kristen swallowed back a mouthful of stress-barf. "Um, what part?"

Massie stepped closer. Kristen could smell her guava Glossip Girl lip gloss. "Have you been *cheating* on me?"

"Yup!" Layne announced with maniacal pleasure. "She sure has!"

"You didn't *know*?" Dune burst out laughing, gripping his stomach for effect.

Massie glared at Kristen, her moistening eyes speaking volumes.

"It's not like that," Kristen pleaded.

"It's *not*?" Layne smirked. "'Cause it kinda is."

"Layne!"

Dune kept laughing. Kristen huffed at him, wishing he were still on the heart-shaped island.

"Have you been helping *her* get Dempsey?"

"Yup!" Layne announced again.

Massie reached for the door, her hand shaking.

"Are you guys a Mariah Carey song?"

Kristen shook her head no, dreading the alpha's next words.

"Because you *belong together*." She threw open the door and slammed it behind her.

"Krist-mas," Marsha called from the kitchen. "Is someone here?"

Before Kristen could answer, the door flew back open. "Forgot my bag." Massie grabbed the handle of her suitcase.

"Oh, and *this*!" She lifted her duplicate key and gouged a huge slit in Layne's cellophane wrapping. An avalanche of Wonka goodies spilled to the parquet floor. "Now we've both been stabbed." The door slammed for the last time.

"Krist-mas?"

"No, Mom!" Kristen snapped.

Layne dropped to her knees and began scooping up the candy. "I can't believe you let her do that to me!"

"You're blaming *me*?" Kristen began to tremble. "And Dune, I can't believe you told her about me and Layne?"

"Why?" He rolled his eyes like it was no big deal. "You should be allowed to have other friends."

"Yeah!" Layne jammed a handful of gobstoppers into the basket.

"I was protecting the Witty Committee," she barked, no longer caring who knew what.

"You were not, Scott!" Layne tugged the shark tooth and stomped her gold high-top. "You were protecting *yourself*!" she yelled, echoing Kristen's exact thoughts from earlier that week. Layne scooped up her wounded basket with one hand and flipped Kristen a sequin-covered bird with the other. "It's been real." She opened the door. "Real pointless." She slammed it shut.

"Krist-mas?"

"It's okay, Mom!"

"Hey." Dune pointed toward the hallway. "Was that my necklace?"

Kristen nodded yes while tears rolled down her cheek.

"You lied?"

She nodded again.

"Layne, wait up!" Dune called, slamming the door behind him.

"Krist-mas." Marsha hurried in from the kitchen. "Are you sure everything's okay?"

Kristen burst out in tears. And then sobs. And then howls. A giant snot bubble pulsed from her nose as she tried to breathe. Thankfully, two salmon-smelling, mismatched oven mitts grabbed her and rocked her like everything was going to be okay. Even though it so wasn't.

Rush hour traffic was worse that usual.

Or maybe it just seemed that way because Massie's mind was speeding and the Range Rover was not. Through her tears, red brake lights blurred like they were being examined through a shifting kaleidoscope.

Is loyalty too much to expect from a best friend? How about honesty? Or . . . loyalty!

"You already said loyalty," Isaac, her driver, kindly noted.

"Oh." Massie sniffled, realizing she must have been talking aloud. "I just can't believe she's friends with *Layme*!"

"What's wrong with *Layne*?" Isaac's caring blue eyes found hers in the rearview mirror. "Claire thinks the world of her."

Massie curled up against the door. "Nawt the point." She pinky-dabbed a mascara-booger and wiped it under the tan leather seat. "The point is, she never *told* me."

"What would you have said if she had?"

"Well, we'll never know now, will we?" Massie sniffled.

Isaac snickered, not quite buying it. "So are you upset that she and Layne are friends or that she didn't tell you?"

The car inched forward.

"Both." Massie wiped her cheeks. "And the fact that Layne is stealing my friends. And that she likes Dempsey. And that she'll probably get him now that she has Claire *and* Kristen on her side. And that I'm supposed to know everything about everyone and I didn't know this. And that being excluded from a secret makes me an LBR, especially since the secret was about me!"

"Massie," Isaac began with that tone he saved for his "things will be better in the morning" lectures.

"Whatevs," she cut him off. "I don't want to talk about it anymore." *With you!* she added silently.

Massie speed-texted Alicia.

Massie: ? r u doing? ☺

She took a deep, calming breath while she waited for a response, thankful that she could mask her despair behind an emotionally ambiguous font and a smiley face.

Alicia: Homework. ☹

Massie tried Dylan next but got no response. And then Claire who—*shocker*—was IM-studying with Cam for the third night in a row.

Gawd, was nothing sacred? She swatted her BFFWC key chain as if her pitiful loneliness were all its fault. Hadn't they pledged "PC support, day or night"? And wasn't now night?!

Massie leaned forward. "Rivera estate," she muttered weakly.

Isaac craned his neck to face her. "Don't you have school-work?"

"Yeah," she breathed against the window. "Social studies. And I need Alicia's help."

Mrs. Rivera greeted Massie warmly, almost like she'd been expecting her. "Alicia is in the dance studio." She gestured toward the back garden with a perma-tanned arm, the smell of freesia sprinkling off her like fairy dust.

"Doing homework?"

She ran her long red fingernails through her damp dark hair. "I doubt it."

Adrenaline prickled Massie's spine like a bee sting. Something was off. She could tell. And it rubbed her like an itchy label in a new sweater.

Denying her instincts, Massie hurried outside as if nothing was wrong. As if she and Alicia hadn't been fighting all week. As if pretending everything was normal could actually make it that way.

Jingling along the flagstone path, Massie was feeling little and sad. Almost flulike. Her head throbbed. Her eyes burned. And her stomach was closed for business.

Swollen from crying, yet out of tears, she was driven by the primal need to be comforted by her best friend. To have her sorrow validated. To hear from someone other than Bean that Kristen was two-faced; that Dempsey would never like Layne; and that in a billion years, Alicia would *never* do anything that backstabbingly backstabbing to her.

If Massie could just hear those things, her alpha spirit

would soar once again and Isaac would be right. Tomorrow would be a better day.

Festive whooping from the song "Live Your Life" escaped through the open windows of the garage-size dance studio. Alicia had obviously finished her homework. Meaning, she'd be able to focus 110 percent on Massie.

Ignoring the DO NOT DISTURB sign, Massie thumb-pressed the iron handle. But the door was locked. "Leeesh!" she called over Rihanna's pinched robotic voice. But the song was too loud.

"Leeeeesh!" She slammed the heart-shaped knocker.

The music stopped suddenly. The sound of feet scrambling across the hardwood floor was as unmistakable as the shushing.

Ehmagawd! A surprise party!

Had the Kristen betrayal thing been part of the setup? Had Dylan been told to ignore her call? Had Claire been supposed to say she was IM-studying with Cam? Was Isaac in on it too? That had to be the case! Nothing else made sense.

Massie fumbled around her GREEN IS THE NEW BLACK tote in search of gloss, cheek stain, and Alicia's dance studio key.

Ha! Who's gonna be surprised now?

"Sur-*prise*!" Massie burst into the studio, her smile ready for its close-up.

"The Curse!" a girl shouted.

Eight shocked faces glared back at her, but she only recognized one of them.

Alicia stepped forward. "Um . . . what are you *doing* here?" She was wearing a crisp white button-down (Ralph, obviously) tucked into denim short shorts with red hearts on the pockets and a matching metallic belt, just like the others.

The invisible fist that had been gripping Massie's stomach all evening reached up and grabbed her throat. Her Socc-Hers uniform, despite its cut-above-ness, was ah-bviously out.

"I thought you said she wasn't on the team," hissed a bony brunette in third position.

"What *team*?" Massie dared.

"The new cheerleaders," offered a curly-headed blonde. "The Heart-Nets."

"*What?*" Massie's eyes begged Alicia's to make this all go away.

"You can totally join if you want," Alicia tried. "I'd love to have you. It's just that . . ." Her voice trailed off.

"*What?*"

"I'm sort of already the alpha." She shifted uncomfortably in her moccasins, which had tiny hearts dangling from its fringes instead of bells.

Massie felt her pores contract.

"I don't mean the alpha in life. Just in dance. You can totally still be the alpha in life. I mean, I *want* you to be. It's just that I'm so into dancing and I would really like to try choreography." She paused. "Actually, if you want to be co-captain you totally can. It would be great. I'll deal with the routine and you can deal with the—"

"Shut up, please," Massie mumbled flatly.

"Huh?"

Alicia seemed slightly taken aback. But come awn. Did she hawnestly think her little speech would make this Brad Pitt–size betrayal hurt any less? The only thing it did was make Kristen's seem a tad less traumatizing.

"Um, Alicia is my name V?" Massie asked loud enough for her teammates to hear.

"No."

"Then why would I follow *U*!?" She bolted into the cool night air, only beating her tears her by a fraction of a second.

Ding.

Dylan rubbed her bare feet together with glee. Derrick was ready for their nightly post-homework text session. If only she'd done her math problems instead of lying on the chaise, stewing over her Massie problems, life would be perfect.

Sucking in the little belly bulge that muffin-topped over her turquoise Cosabella boy shorts, Dylan checked the message.

Derrick: Math blows.
Dylan: Ah-greed!

She kicked her unopened textbook to show she meant it.

The air hung heavy while she waited for another ding. *Was her reply too boring? Should she have tried to sound more upbeat? Did he think she was a triple B?*

Derrick: Mr. Morgan looks like a big toe.

Dylan laughed out loud and then told him so.

Derrick: He's a square root.
Dylan: An odd number.

Derrick: A player eight-er.

Dylan: The ew-y decimal system.

Derrick: LOL!

Dylan felt drained but completely satisfied, like she had just won a grueling tennis match or finished an entire cold-cut combo from Subway. Who was it who'd said, "Every rose has its thorn?" Shakespeare? Oprah? Reebok? As far as she could tell, Derrick's only *thorn* was an ex-crush named Massie Block. And it was very prickly.

Derrick: Cheesy Friday tomorrow @ Slice of Heaven. All u can eay mozrela stix! Wanna hit it after skl??

Dylan's thumping heartbeat practically drowned out Tyra Banks's muffled voice on her sister's flat screen next door. *This was their first official nondetention date!!!*

A swarm of outfits, hairstyles, and conversation topics buzzed through her brain. *Jeans or a dress? Updo or down? Big bones or little ones?* And then the queen bee swooped in, waving a flag that said, FRIDAY NIGHTS ARE FOR SLEEPOVERS AT MY HOUSE, and chasing them all away.

It was so unfair. Massie owned Derrick *and* Friday nights.

Derrick: U still there?

Dylan's thumb hovered over the *y*, longing to answer yes to both his questions. But where would that leave her and

Massie? Not that she should concern herself with someone who had called her a triple B . . . but she did.

Dylan: Hold on. Mom just walked in. Text u back in 5.

She needed to run this problem by someone, but her someone *was* the problem. So she opted for the next best thing.

"Mommmmmm." Dylan padded down the rose petal–covered carpet.

"In here, Dyl Pickles," Merri-Lee called from her bathroom.

Dylan slid the frosted glass door open and stepped into what felt like a gardenia-scented disco ball. Every wall, cabinet, and appliance was made of mirror, right down to the custom toilet. It reflected Dylan, from every angle, along with her mother, who, unfortunately, was naked and slipping into a bubble-filled tub. Out of pure desperation, Dylan perched herself on the edge, next to the flickering pink candle.

"Mmmmmmmm." Merri-Lee closed her eyes and sank into the white froth. "What's up?" she mumbled like she was talking in her sleep.

"Um." Dylan suddenly realized she had no idea how to explain her situation. Only a member of the PC could possibly understand. "You know how you took Jennifer Aniston's side during her split with Brad?"

Merri-Lee's green eyes shot open. "Why? Is Angie's publicist here again?"

"No." Dylan gestured for her mother to lie back down. "I was just wondering if you would have taken her side if she'd told you she was over Brad before Brad hooked up with Angie."

"That shameless PR team! They're using you to get to me, aren't they?"

"No, Mom, I swear." Dylan rolled her eyes, her frustration reflected across the bathroom from every angle. "It's one of those moral-type questions some friends were playing at school, and I wanted to see what you'd say."

"Oh, okay. Start over." Merri-Lee inhaled deeply, ready to concentrate.

"Let's say Jennifer and Angie were best friends, and then Jennifer broke up with Brad, and *then* Angie started liking him. Would that be bad?"

Merri-Lee rubbed sea salt on her arm while considering this. "Not *as* bad, I suppose. Why? What do you know? Do you have a source?"

"*No!*" Dylan snapped. "I just want to know if sometimes it's okay to choose a boy over your friends." She paused. "You know, if that boy's available."

Merri-Lee turned off the water. "I don't think so."

Dylan's heart nosedived. "So you should choose your friend?"

"No."

"The boy?"

"Neither." Merri-Lee shrugged as if it were all so simple.

"Huh?"

"You shouldn't have to choose. A good friend wouldn't intimidate you and a good guy wouldn't pressure you."

Merri-Lee lifted her wet hand and placed it on Dylan's knee. "You deserve both."

"Thanks, Mom." Dylan kissed her mother's dark roots.

Now she knew exactly what to text Derrick. It wasn't going to be easy. But it would be right.

Sleep was nawt an option. It required relaxation, mental clarity, and steady breathing. None of which Kristen had.

"Ugh!" She kicked the covers in frustration.

"Re-owww." Beckham leapt to the shag carpet and zipped under the bed.

Great. Now the cat was mad at her too.

Typically Kristen was an alpha problem solver. But tonight, she couldn't decide which problem to solve first, let alone *how* to solve it. Prioritizing was impossible. Each dilemma was crucial and needed immediate fixing.

There was:

1) Get Dune to forgive her for lying about the necklace.
2) Get Massie to forgive her for lying about Layne.
3) Get Layne to forgive her for denying their friendship.
4) Get Massie to forgive her for not honoring the pledge. (*"PC support day or night!"*)
5) Get Layne to forgive her for not honoring her promise (to help her get Dempsey).
6) Get Alicia to forgive her for ignoring her all night. (Eleven missed calls!)

7) Get Beckham to forgive her for keeping him up past his bedtime.

She considered all seven. Even if she knew which one to tackle first it wouldn't matter. Everyone was fast asleep. E-mailing apology appetizers was the only option.

Dune,
Sorry I lied about the necklace. Didn't want u 2 know I lost it. Didn't know Layne found it. Please forgive me.
XOX,
K

Kristen kissed the computer screen for luck and hit send.

Massie,
Sorry I lied about being friends with Layne. I know u don't like her and I didn't want u to be mad. Which is funny (not in a ha-ha way in an ironic way) cuz now u r. Also sorry I didn't help you get Dempsey or honor our pledge. I will start doing both tomorrow. Please forgive me.
XOX,
K

Kristen kissed the screen twice for extra luck and hit send.

Layne,

Sorry I didn't defend you in front of Massie. U know how she can be. Also sorry I didn't work harder to help u get Dempsey. I was trapped in the middle. We made a promise and I will honor it tomorrow. Please forgive me.

XOX,

K

Kristen kissed the screen one last time and hit send. She had done everything she could right now. The only person left to contact was Dempsey and ask him, straight up, who he liked. But that would have to wait until morning.

Of all the conversations, his would have made the most sense to have via e-mail or text. After all, asking a boy to choose between your best friends can be awkward. But for some reason Kristen wanted to see him when she asked.

Or maybe she just wanted to see him.

Suddenly, everything went quiet.

After lying in fetal position, listening to motivational audio books for three and a half hours, the battery on Massie's iPod died . . . just like everything else that mattered.

She kicked the covers off her aching body and tried to sit up. But vertigo—from crying on an empty stomach—had left her weak and dizzy. Massie collapsed back on her salt-stained purple pillowcase, unable to escape the weight of hopeless desperation.

Adversity was not new to her. In the last year she had triumphed over a Clique-crasher, a cheating Fannish beta, unrequited crushes, a Spanish boy-snatcher, lip-kiss anxiety, a lost movie role, expulsion, an eighth-grade alpha, a boy invasion, class in a trailer, a job in the Hamptons, one week in Kissimmee, and a boyfast. But *this* was different.

Today, all of her friends had betrayed her at the same time. Claire had abandoned her for Cam. Kristen for Layne. Alicia for the Heart-Nets. And Derrington for some mystery beta. All she had left was Dylan, who refused to answer her phone. Oh, and Dempsey, who still hadn't thanked her for the get-well package she'd left outside his door. She had become a human headband, something everyone obsessed over and then tossed.

A fresh stream of tears pooled in her eyes. It was painful

to think of the countless hours she'd spent trying to keep the Pretty Committee on top. The homework missed. The plans hatched. The money spent. The clothes bought. She'd opened up her heart, her bedroom, and her closets to these girls. And despite the countless efforts to hold them back and keep them from moving on, they still . . . *OMG*.

Massie shot up like the waking dead. Something about all this seemed familiar.

"Bean!" She pulled the black pug onto her lap and stroked her tiny head. "Remember you went through that phase of not wanting to go for a walk?"

The puppy sighed.

"I thought it was the cold sidewalks so I bought you those mint green Gucci booties and the white poncho. I sang to you. I gave you Kobe beef treats. And I even got you a pedicure. But you still didn't want to go. Nothing worked until I got you that long leash. Remember?"

Bean looked lovingly at Massie with wet black eyes.

"You just needed more space."

Once again, Massie's spirits plunged like Pam Anderson's necklines. She started crying again.

"But why do *they* want space from me? I gave them *everything*." She sobbed herself empty.

By 2:30 a.m., Massie's breathing had steadied. She had run out of tissues and tears. Her face had the bloat of someone who'd eaten salty movie popcorn at 35,000 feet. Yet her insides had never felt emptier. Any more wallowing and she'd lose her beauty, the only thing she had left.

Massie opened her purple glitter notebook and reviewed the key notes she had taken before her battery died.

AUDIO BOOK #1
How to Make People Like You in 90 Seconds or Less
By: Nicholas Boothman
Key point: The best way to make a person like you is to make yourself be like that person.

AUDIO BOOK #2
25 Ways to Win with People
By: John C. Maxwell & Les Parrott Ph.D.
Key point: Compliment people in front of others. Encourage their dreams.

AUDIO BOOK #3
How to Get What You Want
By: Zig Ziglar
Key point: Set goals.

The last one was easy. Her goal was to get her friends back without looking desperate. The rest would play out in a well-crafted text message. Because the only things Massie was willing to face in the next twelve hours while she pretended she was too sick to go to school were a cucumber eye mask, a bottle of Visine, and her mother.

After several drafts and several more hours, Massie's heartfelt plea was complete.

Dear Alicia, Claire, Dylan, and Kristen,

I understand why you strayed. And I forgive you. I'll forget the past if you will. Let's go back to the way things were. If you agree, which I know you will, show up for our regularly scheduled sleepover tomorrow night. We're closing the pool for the winter. Let's crank the heat to 100 degrees and have one last dunk. See ya then. It's gonna be hawt! ☺

P.S. I won't be at school tomorrow because I ate bad sushi. But I'll be fine for the pool party. Don't be late. ☺ ☺ ☺

Massie hit send and instantly felt a billion times better. She recalled that proverb, Forgiveness is next to Gawdliness . . . or was that cleanliness? Either way, she embodied both. And she did it without having to throw out a bunch of desperate-sounding compliments or hollow dream encouragements. No offense, motivational speakers, but when it came to "making friends and influencing people," there was only one true expert.

And she was exhausted.

"No texting at the table," Marsha insisted, dumping two spoonfuls of sugar in her red mug.

"I'm not *texting*, I'm reading. And this isn't the table, it's the breakfast counter. And you're not even sitting with me—you're standing by the coffeemaker!"

"All technicalities." Marsha kissed her daughter on the head. "Maybe if you shared whatever it is that has you so captivated I'd understand." She moved the crumpled *New York Times* and half-eaten bowl of Cheerios aside to make room for her mug, then sat on the stool next to Kristen. Her nurse's uniform smelled like antibacterial soap.

"It's nothing. Just a text from Massie," Kristen insisted, trying to read. "Just the details for tonight's sleepover. I guess she forgives me." She smiled with her entire body. Her mom-approved mustard crew-neck wool sweater stopped itching. And her tired eyes ceased to burn. She had not been exiled from the Pretty Committee! All was forgiven!!!

"I knew she would." Marsha checked the clock on the microwave. "I better go." She slung a worn black leather tote over her shoulder. "Does this mean Isaac will be picking you up, or do you need a ride?"

Kristen chugged her orange juice. "Isaac," she lied, knowing Massie was taking a bad-sushi day.

Really, she was hoping to tag along with Dempsey and ask which girl he liked. But first she needed to change out of last year's church sweater.

The elevator doors banged shut. Peering through the peephole, Kristen made absolutely sure her mom was gone and then slipped on Massie's old turquoise-and-brown striped Trina Turk sweater minidress. As luck would have it, her ex-Socc-Hers moccasins matched perfectly. She yanked off the bells, stuffed the "before" clothes in her Hedgehog LeSportsac gym bag, gave Beckham a big kiss on the head, and bolted.

It was a new day.

Dempsey was standing outside her apartment, balancing on crutches when she opened the door. His ah-dorable disheveled-chic cargos, worn-in burgundy Harvard tee, and mirrored aviators caught her off guard. He looked like a J. Crew model without the scarf.

"Ehmagawd, *sticks*?" She heard herself giggle nervously.

"Yeah." He blush-nodded. "Ankle fracture. My soccer career is over."

"Awww, I'm so sorry." Kristen tried to look sad while her mind filled with questions. *Does he think I look cute in this dress? How cute? Sister cute or model cute?*

"How are you getting to school?" he asked, pressing the elevator button with the bottom of his crutch. "Wanna ride with my mom and I?"

My mom and me!!!!

"Um . . . I dunno . . . maybe," she stammered, knowing she'd never pull off a heart-to-heart with his mother around.

The elevator doors squeaked open.

Dempsey hobbled inside and sigh-leaned against the back wall for support.

Kristen quickly pressed *L*, trying to appear helpful. The elevator began to dip. Impulsively, she darted forward and hit stop. A bell rang, but neither of them looked the least bit scared.

"What're ya doin'?" he chuckled, amused.

"Um." Kristen's dropped her bags on the ground and tucked her blond hair behind her ears. "I kinda need to ask you something."

Intrigued, he raised his eyebrows like a CW hottie. Cheerios churned in Kristen's stomach. Why was she so nervous? This was about Massie, Layne, and Dempsey. This had *nothing* to do with her. Still, she couldn't seem to come right out and ask.

"So," she managed to say. "Let's play a game."

"You wanna play a *game*?" he said to the flashing emergency light.

"Yeah, it's called Who Would You Rather. I give you choices and you tell me who you'd rather lip-kiss."

"Okay?" he asked like he was helping himself to one of her potato chips.

Kristen wished she had the guts to come right out and ask him. But she didn't want to know the truth. Not yet. Because no matter who he chose, one of her friends would get hurt. And she'd have to break it to them.

"Serena or Blair?" she asked, hitting snooze on the inevitable.

"Blair," he stated like it was obvious.

Hmmmm. He chose the brunette. That boded well for both Layne and Massie, though not Kristen. Not that it mattered.

"Hilary Duff or Vanessa Hudgens?"

"Hudgens."

Another brunette.

"Ms. Dunkel or Principal Burns?" Kristen giggled at her own joke.

"Ugh!" He wince-waved the notion away like it was bad BO.

"You okay in there?" Willard called up from the lobby.

"Yup," Kristen snapped, annoyed by the interruption.

"The maintenance crew should have you out in a jiff," he shout-cough-choked.

"'Kay," Kristen answered. She couldn't hit snooze any longer. It was go time.

Flashing orange lights illuminated the numbers above their heads, their rhythm frenzied and anxious, just like Kristen's heart. Still, she glared up pensively, as if pondering something utterly profound. "Hmmmm." She tapped her bottom lip.

"One."

Tap.

"More."

Tap.

"Question."

Tap. Tap.

"How 'bout . . . uh, I dunno. . . ." *Tap. Tap. Tap. Tap. Tap.* "Layne or . . ." *Tap. Tap.* "Mmmmassie?"

"Seriously?" He cocked his head in a "do you *really* mean that" sort of way.

Kristen nodded that she absolutely did.

Her body buzzed with suspense. His answer would be life changing. She wasn't sure how. Or for whom. Just that it would be.

"Ew," Dempsey said flatly, eyeing his sock-covered foot.

The elevator jolted suddenly, then began to descend.

"*Ew?*" Kristen heard herself screech.

"No." He lifted one of his crutches and poked her calf. "*You.*"

She peered at the lenses of Dempsey's mirrored sunglasses, trying to picture Massie and Layne with a guy like him. But all Kristen could see was herself.

The elevator doors opened quickly.

Too quickly.

And there was Dune. Standing there. Looking cozy-cute in a brown Hurley sweatshirt, a black wool cap, and deliciously faded jeans. He was holding a bouquet of crispy fall leaves bound by a shark-tooth necklace and his sweetest smile.

Ehmagawd, had Dune heard their conversation?

Kristen's cheeks ignited at the thought. Or was it the word *you* stirring in the burnt coffee–scented air?

"Is everyone okay?" Willard asked, his neck meat trembling with concern. "Because, you know, that's never happened before."

"We're cool," Dempsey promised with a reassuring grin.

"Your parents aren't going to sue, are they?"

"Not today," Dempsey joked.

Relieved, Willard shuffled to his desk to greet the UPS deliveryman.

"Dune, what are you *doing* here?" Kristen asked, still inside the elevator. Dempsey's confession had evaporated into a cloud that was now raining tension and guilt all over her.

"I thought we could double to school." Dune pointed at the gold beach cruiser propped against the outside of the building.

The doors began to shut.

Dempsey stuck his crutch out and stopped them before they closed. He hobbled out.

"Fun game," he mumbled as he passed. "Even though I lost."

"No. Wait!" Kristen called, aware that Dune was standing beside her holding a fistful of forgiveness-leaves in the same way one might notice the hum of an air conditioner.

"Yeah?" Dempsey turned, grinning hopefully.

A tsunami of relief washed over her entire body.

And that's when she knew for sure. Dempsey had turned into a serious crush. The kind of crush that kicks you out of the driver's seat and grabs hold of the wheel. The kind that shuts off the GPS and takes you down a different road. The kind that reminds you that crushes don't always follow the rules. And sometimes they don't make sense. They make *non*sense. And trying to force them or deny them is like trying to wear a maxi-dress when you're four feet tall. Just because you want it to work doesn't mean it's going to. And sometimes, the less popular choice—the one nobody will approve of but you—is a perfect fit.

"What is it?" Dempsey pressed.

"Uh." Kristen's words dissolved in her mouth like a Listerine breath strip. "See ya later."

Dempsey held his hopeful gaze, as if there might be more. "That it?"

"Yup," Kristen chirped, stiffly chipper.

He smiled like his mouth had been glued shut, then turned to leave. Her heart gripped onto his good leg, and he dragged it into the chilly morning air.

"Ready?" Dune asked once Dempsey was gone.

"Yup," she chirped again.

"Heyyyyyy," called a familiar voice from the open window

of a Lexus. The car pulled up in front of the building. "Wanna ride?"

"*Layne?*" Kristen squinted even though she had perfect vision. Was that really an orange sequin–covered bathing cap on her head? "What are *you* doing here?"

"I heard Massie ate bad sushi." She sounded pleased. "I thought you might need a ride."

So you're not mad? Kristen asked with furrowed eyebrows as she and Dune walked toward the car.

"Unless you're still too embarrassed to be seen with me," she snickered, half joking but half not.

"I was never too—"

"S'okay." Layne smiled, then leaned her shimmering head out the window even further and whispered, "Just talk to him for me and all will be forgiven."

Kristen's intestines dropped an inch. And then her LeSportsac vibrated with a text message.

Massie: Reminder. Tonight at my house. Hope 2 c u there.

Kristen dropped the phone in her bag. She had never felt more wanted and less happy about it in her entire life. What was she supposed to do *now*?

A) Pretend she liked a surfer who hated soccer and called her friends OCDivas?

B) Pretend Layne still had a chance with Dempsey?

C) Pretend Massie still had a chance with Dempsey?

D) Pretend she and Dempsey had never had that conversation and avoid him like trans fat?

E) Pretend she didn't feel the same way about him?

F) Pretend her own feelings didn't matter so everyone else could be happy?

G) Pretend she'd ever have a friend in the greater New York area again if she didn't choose A through E?

H) Pretend she also ate bad sushi, run upstairs, crawl under her covers, and stay there until she could figure out what to do next?

Without another word, Kristen gripped her stomach and chose H.

Dylan padded across the chilly grass in her brown lace-up Nomads and yellow terry beach tunic, questioning her decision with every crunchy step.

Was it smart to choose the pool party over a movie with Derrick? Was Massie's apology text enough to cancel out her "triple B" comment? And, the biggest question of all . . . Was she going to regret this?

An oasis loomed in the near distance, illuminated like a bonfire on a dark deserted beach.

Steam rose in wavy ribbons. Floating candles cast flickering shadows against the trees. Five brown-and-gold Louis Vuitton inflatable rafts were tethered to steps in the shallow end next to a floating tray stocked with smoothies. And Massie sat alone on the diving board wearing a Pucci silk robe and a matching head scarf. She was dragging her bare foot back and forth in the water, gazing dreamily at her toe-wake.

Dylan inhaled sharply as she stepped out on the deck and into the pale light. "Hey," she called softly.

Massie lifted her chin with an elated smile. Then, like the mini-roll of belly fat Dylan often tried to push up toward her boobs, it fell.

"What's Derrington doing here? This is girls only." The alpha hurried toward them.

"He invited me to a movie, but I wanted to hang with you. So I brought him," Dylan managed, taming her bucking nerves like a seasoned jockey on a bucking bronco.

"Ehma—*no way*. *You're* the girl he's been hanging out with?"

"Why do you sound so surprised?" Dylan snapped, refusing to be degraded for one more second.

"Because he likes me."

"Not anymore," Dylan stated evenly.

"Ladies, no need to fight over me," Derrick tried to joke.

But the girls were locked in a serious stare-down.

"Puh-lease. That's like trading cashmere for chenille." Massie lifted her eyebrow in a "take *that*" sort of way.

Dylan's hands started to quake. Her breathing became choppy. And rage exploded from her like a compressed whitehead. *"I'm chenille?"*

"If the size eight fits . . . " Massie smirked.

"Well, if I'm chenille, you're Lycra!"

"How am *I* Lycra?"

"Because you hold everyone back!"

Derrick snickered.

Massie's mouth dropped open like a shocked emoticon.

"It's true. You're control-top pantyhose." Dylan began to spill like uncontrollable diarrhea. The only way to find relief was to let it all out. "You try to run everyone's lives and keep us all down so you stay on top."

"Opposite of—"

"Oh yeah?" Dylan stepped forward, realizing for the first time that she was at least an inch taller than Massie. "Then why wouldn't you let Alicia help choreograph? She's a much better dancer than you. And why don't you let us have friends outside the PC? And why won't you lift the hold on Derringt— Derrick?"

"Derrick?" Massie giggled.

"Yeah, that's his *name*."

"Yeah!" He kicked a pebble into the pool for emphasis.

"Why would you want to be with someone that immature?"

"Why did *you*?"

"Oh, so you only like him because I did?"

"Hey, I'm not immature!" Derrick pouted.

"No, I like him because you *don't*!" Dylan blurted. Then, like a rainbow after a storm, everything around her felt magical. It was that tingly uplifting feeling that came with knowing you were 100 percent right. "If you still liked him, I would stay away. Because *I'm* a good friend. But you're over him. You like Dempsey now. You told me, like a billion times. So what's the big deal?"

Massie inhaled deeply. "So did you bring him to rub this in my face?"

"No." Dylan smiled confidently. "I brought him so you could remove the hold." She tilted her head toward the twenty-five thousand gallons of water beside them.

"Seriously?" Massie's amber eyes darted from Dylan to Derrick, then back to Dylan.

Dylan nodded yes.

"Fine." Massie shrugged, like she didn't care a bit. With a forceful push, she slapped her hands against Derrick's bare back and shoved him in.

Dylan was about to thank her when she felt the alpha body bump the right side of her body. "Ahhhhhhhhh!" She fell into the pool with a sloppy splash. Warm liquid filled her boots and saturated the fibers of her terry cloth tunic. No matter how hard she fought, the weight of her wardrobe was dragging her down.

"Sinking!" she spat.

Instantly, Derrick was at her side gripping her armpit. It was more romantic than Blair and Nate's season one aqua-kiss.

"Happy?" Massie peered down at them as they reached for the edge. "The hold has been lifted."

Dylan panted.

"Now you're *both* free."

"*Both?*" Dylan peeled a slop of red hair off her forehead.

"Yup." Massie put her hands on her hips. "No more Lycra. Hang wherever. Now get out of my pool."

"Come awn, Massie." Dylan hardly recognized the desperation in her own voice. "Let's just—"

"Go!" Massie turned away. "My *friends* will be here any minute."

Dylan's stomach lurched. She dipped her cheeks in the water to hide her tears. There was no point in appealing to Massie now. She was hurt and embarrassed—an explosive combination. Instead, Dylan stomped across the grass, dripping water and leaking tears while Derrick sloshed along beside her.

"Why can't I have *both*?" she heard herself whimper once they were back on the dark lawn.

"Because"—Derrick nudged her playfully—"maybe I'm all you need."

Dylan sniff-giggled. The tingly rainbow reappeared. Only this time it was Derrick—her brand-new ah-dorable boyfriend—who was right.

Lying flat on her back against the hard, scratchy surface of the diving board, Massie imagined she was in a glass coffin. Her Pucci head scarf had unraveled slightly, and dark hair fanned out around her head like Sleeping Beauty's. Only this tale would not end with a handsome prince. Or a kiss. Or a happily-ever-after. It was forty-nine minutes too late for that. No one had come to her sleepover. She was already dead.

The stars, elegant crystal beads on a boundless black dress, were no longer something to behold. They were something to envy. Surrounded by others . . . looking down on the world . . . admired; how *she* used to be.

At 7:55 p.m., she had made a list of possible reasons why the universe had heralded Massie Block the victim for this unprecedented and mighty social eclipse. By 8:02 p.m. she had completed the list . . . and more.

REASON FOR ECLIPSE	SOLUTION	STATUS
Gawd wants me to suffer so I can rise from the ashes to teach people how to overcome.	Through prayer, remind Gawd that he already gave that job to Oprah. And that she's doing a great job.	Completed at 8:13 p.m. Bean Block was a witness. See ↘ smoothie paw print. 🐾
Possible cell service outages kept Kristen, Claire, and Alicia from getting my text invite.	Call all service providers and investigate outages in tri-state area over last 24 hours.	Completed at 8:28 p.m. Bean Block was a witness. See ↘ smoothie paw print. 🐾
I never got pigeon-pooped. Maybe it really is good luck?	Place a spicy tuna roll on my shoulder to attract a pigeon, then hope for poop.	Completed at 8:33 p.m. Removed roll when realized there are no pigeons at night. Only bats. Bean Block was a witness. See ↘ smoothie paw print. 🐾
The soccer fans put a curse on me when they called me "the Curse."	Ask housekeeper Inez how to remove it. (She's ah-mazing with stains.) Then curse them back times ten.	Must wait until next soccer game.
I really am Lycra, and now everyone is mad at me.	Become an elastic waistband and give a little.	No.

Massie squeezed her eyes shut, pouted, and then moaned. The tiny voice in her head sounded like a hungry kitten's sorry meow. But no tears came. So she tried again. And again, certain that people who lost their friends were expected to sob uncontrollably and that if she did, the PC would sense her despair and stampede toward her with open arms.

But no matter how many times she pictured Bean getting hit by an SUV, her eyes refused to cooperate.

It wasn't like Massie didn't feel heartbroken over her social expiration. She *did*. Her heart felt like a lone helium balloon, drifting endlessly with nothing to anchor it. And it wasn't like she didn't *want* to be a good friend. She *did*. It was the most important role in her life. She just didn't want to change who she was to do it. And who she was *was* controlling. And for years the girls had wanted that. They'd needed it. They'd looked to her for it. She'd given them structure. Confidence. Wardrobe guidelines. Social counseling. A place to belong and people to belong to. And up until now, no one had complained.

Sure, Massie could have let Alicia choreograph the Socc-Hers, but then it wouldn't have been *her* team. She could have released Derrington earlier, but then she wouldn't have had a fallback guy if Dempsey chose *Layme*. She could have been nicer to Kristen about her friendship with the LBR, but then everyone would have thought it was okay to keep secrets from her. And a good leader had to set boundaries.

And then there was Claire. The only person she didn't Lycra. Maybe that was because Claire had made it clear from the very beginning that she couldn't be controlled, especially when it came to her extra-Cam-rricular activities. So why bother, especially when there were so many others who required her services?

Massie tried to cry again. But that was soooo last night, this morning, and this afternoon. Now she felt angry, taken for granted, and used. She sat up and twirled her purple hair streak. Maybe it could buy her some new, better friends. . . .

"Hey," said a kind voice.

Massie turned. Claire and Cam were standing by the shallow end.

"I wasn't sure if you'd still be here." Claire helped herself to a smoothie and sipped. "We were just at my house playing Jenga." She shrugged, slightly embarrassed. "Family game night."

"I crashed." Cam smiled.

"Literally." Claire giggled.

"Hey." He nudged her. "That was Todd's fault, not mine. He sucks at Jenga."

"No, you do."

"No, you do."

"No, you do!"

"Truce?"

"Truce."

They giggle-bumped fists.

Massie rolled her eyes.

"Where is everyone?" Cam lifted the hood of his green

sweatshirt and jammed his hands in the side pockets. "I thought this was a party."

Claire lowered her head and wiggled her bare feet nervously.

"Girls only," Massie snapped, not wanting to explain the poor turnout.

"Um, okay." Cam surveyed the empty pool. "So where are the g—"

"Isn't your brother coming to get you soon anyway?" Claire butted in.

Cam nodded, returning his wilted smoothie to the floating tray.

"It's okay, he can stay," Massie managed, trying to be an elastic waistband. "Everyone already left, so I can open it up to boys now."

"Nah, Harris is probably waiting for me. I should go."

Claire nodded in agreement, then lifted her fist for a farewell knock. "Text you later."

"'Kay." He grinned, his blue eye and green eye scanning her face like it was the horoscope page.

"'Bye Massie." He lifted his palm.

Massie smiled back, feeling the freedom that comes with being open. It felt like falling down a dark shaft. It was nawt for her.

Once they were alone, Claire walked toward her slowly, as if she might bite.

"You okay?" Her blond eyelashes fluttered with concern.

"Given." Massie tightened her head scarf. "Why?"

"Well . . ." Claire lifted her eyebrows at the table of untouched party snacks.

"Never better," Massie lied.

"Cool."

"Cool."

They grinned at each other the way people who are lying and know they're lying grin, their sheepish expressions communicating what their mouths were too embarrassed to say.

"How's the water?" Claire asked.

Massie half smiled. "You tell me," she blurted, then shoved Claire into the steaming pool.

Claire's ill-fitting Tomahawks sweatshirt parachuted around her. "You're dead!"

Ignoring the sad truth of that statement, Massie giggle-ran to the other side of the pool.

Claire hurried up the ladder, the sleeves of her sweatshirt drip-hanging to her knees like ape arms.

Here Massie was, being cackle-chased by her only friend—a girl in an ill-fitting sweatshirt with unkempt toenails—and she couldn't have felt more proud. She wasn't about to compromise her standards to be liked, not even for popularity. After all, wasn't that what Alicia, Kristen, and Dylan had been doing all these years? And look at how unhappy it had made them.

Instead, Massie untied her robe, whipped it playfully at Claire, and then jumped in the pool.

"What are you doing?" Claire asked, still laughing.

"Removing the hold on myself."

Massie lifted her arms like the wings of a phoenix and shot down to the bottom of the pool. Everything was silent except for the muted grumble of the pool filter and her bubble-filled vow to "move on" and "start fresh."

After all, she'd be picking a new Clique on Monday.

CURRENT STATE OF THE UNION	
IN	**OUT**
Lycra	Elastic waistbands
Lyons	Lemmings
New beginnings	Old friends

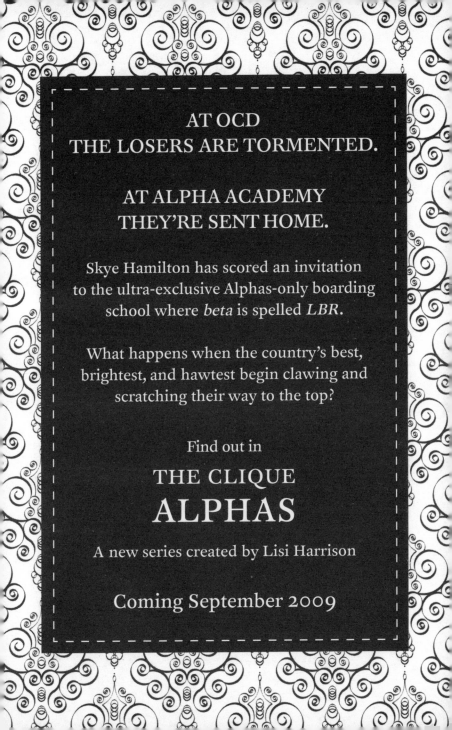

AT OCD
THE LOSERS ARE TORMENTED.

AT ALPHA ACADEMY
THEY'RE SENT HOME.

Skye Hamilton has scored an invitation
to the ultra-exclusive Alphas-only boarding
school where *beta* is spelled *LBR*.

What happens when the country's best,
brightest, and hawtest begin clawing and
scratching their way to the top?

Find out in

THE CLIQUE
ALPHAS

A new series created by Lisi Harrison

Coming September 2009

THIS YEAR'S HAWTTEST ACCESSORY

EHMAGAWD...YOUR FAVE BOOK IS ON DVD!

AH-DORABLE **EXTRAS**

- The Search for the Real Life Pretty Committee
- Ehmagawd! We're Rolling
- The Clique Movie: Tween Couture
- The Clique Movie Casting Contest Winners
- Clique Girlz in the Studio
- Gag Reel

TYRA BANKS PRESENTS
THE CLIQUE

The only thing harder than getting in is staying in

Fashion isn't everything.
It's the *only* thing . . .

POSEUR

When four sophomores with a fierce passion for fashion are put in a class to create their own designer label, they Clash with a capital C. At LA's Winston Prep, survival of the fittest comes down to who fits in—and what fits.

POSEUR

The Good, the Fab and the Ugly

Petty in Pink (coming July 2009)

The stylish and hilarious new series by Rachel Maude.

Welcome to Poppy.

A poppy is a beautiful blooming red flower
(like the one on the spine of this book). It is also
the name of the new home of your favorite series.

Poppy takes the real world and makes it
a little funnier, a little more fabulous.

Poppy novels are wild, witty, and inspiring.
They were written just for you.

So sit back, get comfy, and pick a Poppy.

poppy

www.pickapoppy.com